About the Author

Kefira Zink is a woman of many hats. The wife of a retired soldier, she also has a Bachelor's in sociology and is working on her Master's. In her spare time, she is raising her six children, or playing with her three cats, one dog that thinks it is a cat, and a lizard that thinks it is a dinosaur.

The Trials of AnnaBella Cain

Kefira Zink

The Trials of AnnaBella Cain

Vanguard Press

VANGUARD PAPERBACK

© Copyright 2024
Kefira Zink

The right of Kefira Zink to be identified as author of this work has been asserted by them in accordance with the Copyright, Designs and Patents Act 1988.

All Rights Reserved

No reproduction, copy or transmission of this publication may be made without written permission.
No paragraph of this publication may be reproduced, copied or transmitted save with the written permission of the publisher, or in accordance with the provisions of the Copyright Act 1956 (as amended).

Any person who commits any unauthorised act in relation to this publication may be liable to criminal prosecution and civil claims for damages.

A CIP catalogue record for this title is available from the British Library.

ISBN 978 1 80016 870 1

This is a work of fiction. Names, characters, businesses, places, events and incidents are either the product of the author's imagination or used in a fictitious manner. Any resemblance to actual persons, living or dead, or actual events is purely coincidental.

Vanguard Press is an imprint of
Pegasus Elliot Mackenzie Publishers Ltd.
www.pegasuspublishers.com

First Published in 2024

Vanguard Press
Sheraton House Castle Park
Cambridge England

Printed & Bound in Great Britain

To Krystal McCauley, thank you for all your help editing and your encouragement. To my husband, Brent, thank you for always believing in my dreams. Thanks for lunch and I am so glad you forgot the med keys.

Contents

Part One: The Trials of Humans 11

Part Two: The Trials of the Arena 86

Part Three: The Trials of the Gods 217

Part One: The Trials of Humans

Time is not real. Scientists pretend it is a fundamental law of nature, but they are full of shit. Ask any physicist and they will tell you they have no idea how time works. Sure, they will hem and haw and talk of this theory and that theory. But the truth is they can't tell you how it really works because it is all made up. Any kid who has ever been subjected to the public school education system could tell you that. Why? Because they stare at clocks all day, watching their hands spin around at lightning speed when they need more time or slow to a crawl when there is too much time.

That is what I was doing. Watching the clock. It was warm. Just that perfect June warm where a slight trickle of sweat rolls down your back but the breeze blows and you feel lazy and glorious and like everything is promising but a nap would be perfect. The school's AC was always fritzy, so Ms Campbell had opened the window to let in that breeze. As if it being the last day of school on such a perfect day wasn't bad enough, she had to let that tantalizing breeze in, carrying the sounds and smells of summer break in with it.

I glanced at the clock. Five more minutes until the bell rang and freedom. The freedom of spending the whole summer at Dad's house instead of half at Dad's and half at Mom's. Don't get me wrong, I loved my mom, and summer breaks with her were great. But Dad and I have always just connected better. Some things are the same whether I am at Dad's or at Mom's.

When I was young, they both used the same babysitter, who I thought was cool and fun. But now, both of them would go to work and leave my teenaged self alone with the full freedom to eat junk food and laze all day, or go to the mall with their unlimited credit cards, or have friends over. Both Mom and Dad would come home at night and be very into asking me about my day, listening to me ramble on about whatever random factoid I learned, or movie I watched. They would watch the news with me and have conversations about politics without ever treating me like I am too young, politely teaching me things I didn't know and giving me the time to decide for myself what that means. They both were up for mini-adventures on the weekends, short trips to explore eighteenth century historical sites or wander in a natural forest preserve or drive up past Stephen King's house for no real reason other than something to break up the monotony.

Mom and Dad would even be down to rearrange the court-ordered vacation schedule if Mom's work was taking her someplace cool so I could go with her and we could make a vacation out of it. Like the time we went to the Australian Outback. And they both treat me like I am the most important thing in the whole world to them. Most of my friends can't even get that out of one of their parents, let alone both.

But somehow with Dad it was always different. The conversations more intense, like he was teaching me things without me realizing I was learning. I felt like I was just having a really deep discussion with him. Mom and I had amazing conversations too, but with her, if she was teaching me something, I knew I was being taught, even if I was enjoying the learning. The adventures with Dad seemed less random, or sometimes more. He seemed to instinctively know if I needed to feel wild and free, or grounded and safe, and would work that into our time. I always felt safe with Mom, or wild and free, but she always seemed to need to feel out what I needed more than Dad did.

But none of these things really explains the connection between Dad and me. Mom and I could connect on so many levels I never could with Dad because, well, he's my dad. No matter how cool a dad is, you really can't talk to them about boys or bra shopping or that time of the month without it being a little weird. With Mom, those discussions were never weird. She always made me feel like they were just things we could talk about, even though my friends never felt they could talk about them with their moms or their dads. No matter how many times I examine why

I feel more attached to my dad than my mom, I can never really put my finger on it. I just am.

Looking at the clock after completely psychoanalyzing my relationship with my parents in my head for the millionth time, I expected to see that the bell should be ringing any second. But like I said, time has no real meaning. Only thirty seconds had passed.

Ms Campbell was droning on about something. Glancing around, I didn't think anyone else in my advanced English lit class was paying attention either. What could she really be saying of any importance anyway? In four minutes and thirty seconds, about half the class would be graduated, done with high school completely and going on into the big world as adults, to college or trade school or whatever. The other half were juniors who, having completed this class, had exhausted all of the English classes my high school offered and were going to dual enroll at the local community college to get both high school and college credits or were either finding other ways to fill credits next year.

I was part of the second group, planning on maxing out credits by co-oping. I already worked it out with my guidance counselor. Half my school day, I would come to school and finish the few remaining credits I needed to graduate and the other half I would work with my father at his company and get high school credit for what I learned there. Hence why I was getting the whole summer with Dad. I needed to start my training this summer. Ms Campbell had nothing left to give us in the next... ugh. Four minutes and twenty-five seconds.

I glanced across the room at Lila, my friend who was a senior. She rolled her eyes at me and I knew she was feeling the same anticipation and sense that the clock must have broken. In those four minutes and change, she would be off on her own grand adventure. As soon as school was over, she would picked up by her mother and taken to the airport. She had been accepted to a university in Scotland to study English literature, and would be starting there in the fall, but was going early to have a vacation with her mom and see all the sights in England, Ireland, Wales and Scotland. I almost envied her, studying the Brontë sisters, Jane Austen, Dickens and all the rest right where they wrote their work. But Lila wanted to be a writer, so for her it would be great inspiration. I never really wanted to be a writer, but here we are. Sometimes plans go askew from where we thought we would be.

Looking at Lila reminded me that I was not the only kid in my school who had this dual-home life. Not by a long shot. Lila's mom and dad were not together any more and so she understood the dual-home lifestyle. But my situation was different than hers, really different than the average 'mom and dad got divorced and so now I live with one and see the other on alternating weekends and for half the vacations' type deal. My parents were never married. Even that wouldn't be really strange. Except, my parents never really even knew each other.

I have known my whole life that the only reason my parents had any relationship whatsoever was to create me. And even that relationship was very distant and not what most people would think.

The basic story, as I know it, is this. Mom was kind of in a rough place in life. She wanted a kid. She met my dad. He also was in sort of a rough place and wanted a kid. Neither of them really wanted the type of relationship that was usually the prerequisite to having a kid but neither of them really wanted a donor kid or to adopt. So, they made a pact to do it together. They even went to lawyers and had all the legal custody stuff drawn up before I was even conceived. Then they made me. Even that was very clinical, using invitro fertilization. They weren't even in the same country as each other when my mom got pregnant with me. They did all the normal pregnancy stuff together. Dad was there for Mom's doctor's appointments, and the ultrasounds, and when I was born. But after that, they split their own ways, each taking turns with me as the legal stuff told them to.

That's not to say they never worked together to raise me. If there was ever a time they both needed to be there, they were. When I fell and broke my leg when I was four, Mom called Dad to come to the hospital and they both held my hand, one on each side of my bed. When I had my band concerts in middle school, both Mom and Dad came. High school dances, if I was getting ready at Dad's house, Mom would come over to take pictures too, both of them swapping the good ones with each other once I left. And I never needed something without the two of them working it out together. My parents solved who would pay what for my braces with a ten-minute pleasant phone call. They have always worked together and been completely nice to each other when it came to me. Just, the rest of their lives, they are basically slight acquaintances with no real things in common. They don't hate each other, or even despise each other. They just don't know each other or care to, unless it is about me. So yeah, my parents' relationship is strange to say the least.

Ms Campbell, I think, gave up. She was kinda mumbling now, not really talking to us. And even she had started packing up her things. I looked at the clock again. I had been trying not to stare at the clock because watched pot never boils and all that, but it's hard not to. All the gods damn it… three minutes.

A big wind pushed through the open window. We could hear the kids from the middle school down the block laughing and yelling. They get out fifteen minutes before the high school, so they were already free for the next three months. The middle schoolers must have been running through the soccer field the janitor just mowed because the breeze smelled like fresh cut grass so strong, it made me want lemonade. Ms Campbell looked at the clock herself and then looked at all the bored, anxious faces of English lit students who just wanted to go home. She rolled her eyes and sighed.

"Aw, to hell with it," she said. "Get outta here." Every single student in advanced English lit, except me, ran for the door before she changed her mind. Lila and I had said goodbye at lunch. I understood she would be on a time crunch to make her plane to Scotland and wouldn't have time after school for a lengthy, 'Promise you'll write, or at least SnapChat me' goodbye. As she darted ahead of the crowd out the door, we waved goodbye one more time. I packed up my stuff slowly, knowing Dad would not be here for a few more minutes. I could let the rabble make their way out and then leave without having all the crushing bodies of jocks and preps and cheerleaders forcing their way around me like I don't exist. Because to them, I didn't.

The jocks and preps in school usually ignore the plain, untalented, rather uncoordinated girls who are smart but not debate team, Science Olympiad trophy winning smart. My parents were more or less wealthy for the area, but since I wouldn't buy into all that name-brand, gotta have the latest fad, I'm gonna cry if I get the red plain Iphone instead of the blue Iphone Pro spoiled girl stuff, they lost interest in me as a rich girl friend pretty quickly. Since they couldn't check me into one of their little cliquey boxes, they all kind of just pretended I didn't exist. But I didn't care if I existed to them. This was high school. And as Dad always tells me, in the grand scheme of the world, high school is just one level of purgatory humans have to climb through on the way to either the best, most heavenly delights or the depth of unimaginable hell. The choice of which way we went was up to us. Dad says strange things like that all the time. I think it is why I like him so much.

I should apologize. I haven't introduced myself to you. After the last few weeks, months... How long has it been? Anyway, after the last while spent where I have been, I forget that most people I talk to are not omniscient. My name is AnnaBella Cain. Mom wanted to name me Anna and Dad wanted to name me Bella, so true to my parents' fashion, they compromised. Mom still calls me Anna, and Dad calls me Bella, but when talking to each other they both use my full name. I am currently seventeen years old, and as I said, just finished my junior year of high school. I am the product of two exceptional people.

My mom, Julia McIntosh, is a lawyer for an international human rights activist group. She met Dad between finishing her Bachelor's degree and starting law school and had me directly after law school, while she was working for the group as a legal assistant before being promoted to lawyer. Her work takes her everywhere in the world, and she loves learning about different cultures, religions, food, all of that. And she brings all that home to me. It's fascinating sometimes. Like I said, when I was learning from Mom, I knew I was learning, but still really enjoyed it. Beyond being crazy smart and an impressive, persuasive speaker, Mom is gorgeous. Tall at five foot nine, she is slender but definitely fit, long reddish-brown straight hair, pale, flawless skin and no one who looked at her all done up in her power suit and spike heels would think she ever had a baby.

Dad, on the other hand, looks like some sort of Spanish male model. Tall, muscles but not lunky, jet black hair, olive skin, just the hint of an accent. I always think his accent reminds me of the Italian Riviera but he claims he was born here in the United States. Nick Cain was already a lawyer when he and Mom met. I understood Dad's job a lot less than Mom's. I knew he works as a prosecuting attorney, but he doesn't work for the state or county government. Obviously, this summer, I learned a lot more about Dad's job and find it… interesting. But yeah, that's the reason you are reading this, right? To learn about me and Dad's job?

Anyway, they said to tell you my story. So, I am telling it to you. I will try to remember not to assume you know stuff again, but excuse me if I kinda get wound up in the details. My story is my story, so I gotta tell it my way, right? I want to make sure you know what you need to so you can make your choice.

Anyway, I look nothing like either of them. I am not tall, only five foot three. I am not slender and muscles, pudgier. Not fat or anything, but I won't be modeling for Victoria's Secret any time soon. Mom's perfect reddish-brown and Dad's sleek jet-black hair combined to give me a muddy brown with just enough auburn in it to make dyeing it a pain in the butt. Her bone straight hair plus his beautiful curls? I get just wavy enough to be a mess but not enough to look fashionable and I wake up to my hair looking like a rat's nest most mornings. I did get Dad's fantastic bone structure in my face, with his distinct almond shaped eyes and well-placed cheekbones. I got my mom's full lips that make applying lipstick (when I care to, which is like never) a breeze and her gracefully long fingers.

And they both gave me their eyes. Mom's clear green and Dad's striking blue mixed together to give me both blue and green. Most people would call it hazel but they aren't mixed. My eyes fluctuate in a really cool way between being blue sometimes and green others, and sometimes you can distinctly see both colors in my eyes. Once when I was super pissed, my friend said one of my eyes was very blue while the other was very green. It was weird and kinda freaked them out but went away when I calmed down. So yeah, not hazel eyes exactly. Oops, wound up in the details again. Anyway, that should fill you in on the basics you need to know about me before the story, the 'you aren't omniscient and can't see me' stuff. Back to the story...

By the time I had wound my way out of class, through the throngs of people hugging bye like they don't live two blocks from each other and won't see one another again in like twenty minutes at the mall, and to my locker, the actual dismissal bell had rung. So much for avoiding the crowds... I emptied my locker, waved bye to a select few teachers roaming the halls, but only a few of them seemed to notice. Most of the teachers were trying to shepherd the masses out the door so they could start their break. Eventually, I walked out the front doors of the school into the glorious sunshine.

Usually, I walk home from school to Mom's house, but when it is Dad's time, he picks me up. It is a little bit further, but I could walk to his place too. I think he just likes to savor every minute of his time with me. Either that, or he really likes the appreciative whistles he gets from the dude-boys when they see his bright red Hennessey Venom F5. That's a sports car that looks super cool and a lot like the Batmobile to the uninitiated.

Mom and Dad were weird in another way. Looking at Dad just standing on a street corner, you wouldn't have thought he was a high-powered anything. Jeans and T-shirts with flip-flops were his daily attire. But look at his home, his car, whatever and it all screamed, 'I make a crap ton of money and love to show it'. He lived in a penthouse condo with a doorman, a newer building with floor to ceiling tinted windows on the exterior walls and a small, shared rooftop garden.

Mom was the complete opposite. She had the middle-class standards, an older, single story, three-bedroom, two-bath Craftsman detached home with a fenced-in yard and shutters and flowers on the windowsills. Mom drove a mid-sized, used Kia that was serviceable and she wouldn't trade it in until something on it broke and it was cheaper to replace than fix. But her wardrobe? Stilettoes and power suits, always had red somewhere in the outfit, make-up on point. Even when we went hiking and she was wearing leggings and jogging shoes, her outfits let you know she was the boss and she ain't taking shit from nobody.

I spotted Dad's car (not hard) in the carpool pick-up lane. Dad was leaning against the side of the car, tipping his sunglasses to the guys waiting for the school bus who were noticeably drooling. As soon as I got to the car, all his attention focused on me and I could tell he forgot everyone else existed. He looked at me like that all the time, like the world could literally be burning around him but all he would care about is if I am smiling. I loved that.

"Bella Bella!" he cried. "You're free."

I laughed as we both got into the car. "Dad, I wasn't in prison or something."

Dad held up his hands as if he was weighing two things against each other. "Prison, public school, eh. Is there really much difference?" He winked at me as he started the motor. I could almost hear the boys at the bus positively moaning as the Venom's engine made itself known. "You can't say the food isn't the same."

Dad gave me a minute to adjust my bookbag around me on the floor of the car, then resumed talking. As he started pulling away from the school, he continued. "Speaking of food, my basic plan for tonight was to grab some Indian on the way to the house for dinner, as a homage to your mom's big trip. Do you want to stop at Mom's before we head that way? Give her a hug goodbye before she leaves on her flight to India tomorrow?"

Mom was taking advantage of the whole summer off of kid duty to spend some time traveling the world for work. I know she factored some fun exploring in there, and had I not been going with Dad for the whole summer, would have either invited me along or curtailed some of the fun bits to be with me, totally unbegrudgingly. I was actually kinda glad she was going, though. She works really hard, doing really important stuff for some really underprivileged people and deserved to have the fun parts of traveling the world too.

"I hugged her bye this morning," I told Dad. "But I also wouldn't mind one more?" I looked at my dad out of the corner of my eye, slyly. Dad winked at me again and turned left out of the school parking lot, towards Mom's house, instead of right towards his. Like I said, no animosity, no fight, just a general complete respect of each other's roles in my life. So weird.

The ride to Mom's house was short, only a few minutes. We pulled in the drive and I hopped out, making quick work of the long driveway to the front porch where Mom was already outside and waiting for us. Wanna make a wager Dad called and said he would swing me around for one last goodbye? A cool twenty says he did. I took the steps up to the porch two at a time and dove right into my mom's open and waiting arms.

She smelled my hair, kissed my forehead. "Mmmm, I love you so much Anna-girl. Be good for your father, OK?" Mom pulled my face into her cupped hands and looked deep into my eyes. "Promise me. Safe? Listen to him?" I nodded and Mom pulled me back into another deep hug.

"Oh! Anna, darling," she continued before I had the chance to wonder why she was being so weird, like going to work with Dad was somehow more dangerous than her going to crazy places in the world where not everyone has basic human rights. "I found some of those chips you like at the store today while I was grabbing plane food, the ones with the strange flavor combinations Dad can never find. They're on the counter in the kitchen. Run grab them so you can have them at his house." She let go of me and raised an arm in a half-wave to Dad, who was meandering slowly up the walk.

As I took off to the kitchen, I could hear my parents' exchanging pleasantries. Their voices got more muddied as I walked through the living room and dining room to the kitchen at the back of the house. Everything looked a little off as I passed through each room. Mom had always had an amazing sense of style and each room of the hundred-year-old Craftsman house had always looked almost period accurate but still was warm and inviting. There were stained glass lamps next to soft, plump couches in muted blues and greens in the living room, an old oak table and sideboard in the dining room, scarred from years of use but polished to a high shine, and all the possible updated cooking tech you could ask for next to the original, handcrafted cabinets in the kitchen.

Mom loved plants too, so there have always been at least one or two blooming things in every room of the house for my whole life. Now, all the furniture was hidden under dust covers and the plants were gone, shipped off to this friend's or that friend's to be cared for while Mom and I were both gone an extended amount of time.

I grabbed the chips off the bare counter, spending an extra minute to see which ones she found. Oh! Steak and onion, those are the best! I opened that bag right away and started munching as I slowly made my way back to the front porch. Mom and Dad seemed like they were having an actual discussion on the porch so I wanted to give them the space to do it. But like, I was also seventeen which means nosy as hell. So, I stopped short of the door, where they wouldn't see me but I could hear them.

"You sure it's safe? I know, I know, I agreed in the initial arrangement, but that's my baby…" Mom was saying.

"Jules, you know I treasure her too. Do you really think I would go through with it if I didn't see some glimmer? Contract be damned, if I had a shadow of a doubt, I would just use my connections to get her an internship at the district attorney's office for next year."

Dad was talking low and with none of the usual carefree, easy breezy attitude he normally spoke with. Intrigued, I moved closer to the front picture window to be able to see them. Dad had placed his hand gently on Mom's shoulder. When was the last time they even touched? I couldn't remember if they ever had.

Mom sighed so deep it was almost a shudder. "I have never, and will never, doubt your absolute love for AnnaBella," she said in a whisper. Then even softer, she said. "But she will come back to me, right? I get one more year, her senior year. You can guarantee that?"

Dad then did the unthinkable in my world. He pulled Mom into a hug. "I promise you will see her again." He pulled back and held Mom with both arms out so he could look in her face. "Listen, I am going to run tests before I take her to the office. I'll do it at home, tonight. You've seen her eyes. It's in there. But I will check how deep. If it's not enough, Plan B. But if it is, she deserves this chance."

What in a bloody Nora were they talking about? Tests? Glimmers? My EYES?! I knew that the court arrangement, made before I was even born, gave my dad the whole summer after I turned seventeen rather than just half, but suddenly I was questioning why. Again. They had told me when I asked years ago that it was to give my dad more time before the end of my senior year, in the assumption that Mom would get all of the summer after graduation to get me ready to go to college, but in light of this conversation I called bull on that answer. What was the real reason?

Dad was still talking. "I will tell her everything tonight, just like we planned. If it goes the way I think, I will take her to the office and start the process. If not, I will still take her there, but it will just be so she knows everything. Just like you, she will know but be able to live her life like normal. If there is nothing there, she deserves the truth. Do you agree?"

Mom and Dad had pulled away from each other, and besides the odd context I didn't get, the talk had turned back into a normal conversation between my parents when they are deciding what is best for me. My mom nodded her agreement, and I decided to make my presence known. This was starting to weird me out too much.

I slammed the screen door a little hard as I walked out, purposely drawing my parents' attention. They both looked at me. Mom looked like she was fighting an urge to cry (OO, send me round the confusion bend a little more, will ya? Mom crying? Mom never cried. Never). Dad looked more serious than I had ever seen him. They both looked up when the screen door slapped closed, and seeing me standing there, on a dime they both changed their demeanor back to the standard for my life with them. Pleasant, cordial, quasi-disinterested in each other but unabashedly all about me.

OK, slight interruption. Just want to make something clear. I am not spoiled. You should know that. When I say my parents make everything about me, I don't mean in the spoiled little brat way where they are permissive parents who give me everything and they think, or let me think, I am more important or deserving than anyone else. They are only all about me in the, 'there is no point in us talking or even knowing each other without AnnaBella' way. My parents both saw to it that I was raised to be thoughtful, modest, and understanding of my privileges as well as gracious and giving. I am not the center of the world, just the center of their relationship. No hovering or pampering, just devoted parents. You good on that? Cool, just making sure. Anyway...

"Bella, baby! Ready to rock this joint?" Dad asked casually, as if he and Mom had not just been on the verge of breaching every unspoken rule of how they interact with each other. "Hug your momma one more time. She is going miss you."

I complied, saying, "Have fun in India, Mom. And South Africa, and Guatemala and..." I frowned. Where else was she going?

Mom laughed. "Minnesota, baby. My last stop is Minnesota." Oh yeah, so random I always forgot that one. We both laughed and hugged tight. Then I let her go and walked away. Excited for the whole summer with Dad, excited to see where he worked and what he did and to start the next part of my life as a semi-adult human (kinda pushing down the freakout about that convo between them), I got in the Venom and waved as Dad drove away.

Fuck. Did Mom know? Does she know now? Does she have a clue that that was maybe the last time I see her before she dies? Think on that a little, will you? Cuz I didn't know. I would have held her tighter, longer if I had. Or would I? Damn it, I don't know. How can they expect you to?

Dad was quiet as we headed into town, away from the suburbs, towards his condo. He lived just on the edge of town, walking distance from Mom's and school, but he bypassed his place to hit up Yasmeen's Takeout for dinner. Finally, he broke the silence. "How much did you hear?" he questioned me, one eye on me, one eye on the road.

"What?" I started. But Dad has this way, I don't get it. Lies kinda die in your throat around him. "A little. A lot. Most of it, maybe all, not sure."

"OK," he said, doing that weird seriousness again. "Let's get dinner, eat, and then I will explain that conversation." I must have looked a little panicky, because Dad laughed, and it broke the tension I had been feeling a little. "It's all good Bella Bella. You aren't in trouble. I won't bite, just a little discussion about life and everything. You know, forty-two and all that."

I relaxed some. Dad was making nerd jokes about good books. Whatever that conversation with Mom was about, it couldn't be all that crazy then. Huh. Wrong again, moose breath.

The rest of the evening went more on the normal side. We got Yasmeen's, took it back to the condo, tossed some gulab jamun at Ricky the doorman on the way up, and then sprawled our treasure hoard of way too much food across the glass dining table, eating a bit of this and a bite of that directly out of the takeout boxes. Plates meant dishes and rock paper scissors for who had to wash up.

We talked the whole time too. It was normal when I came to his house for us to play catch up while eating dinner the first night I was there. I saw Dad every other weekend during the school year, unless something special was going on, so usually we had a lot to tell each other about. I told Dad about babysitting the dog from next door at Mom's house last weekend and how he ate Mom's basket-of-gold flowers. I will be paying Mom back for the emergency vet visit until I am thirty, but the dog was fine. Dad told me about the latest book he had been reading, and that he watched the movie based on the book and was disappointed. He was every time, why did he keep doing that?

What we didn't talk about, I noticed, was the upcoming conversation. We also didn't talk about Dad's work, or me joining him there, or what I would be doing. And we definitely didn't talk about my eyes. If we got even kind of close to any of that, Dad artfully changed the conversation to something else. The soccer championship in Brazil. The rising cost of fuel. The price of tea in China. Anything else.

But then we had eaten all the food we could stuff in, the takeout boxes were cleaned up and stored in the fridge for the next week's worth of lunches. The table was wiped down, floor swept up, and the dining room had been made spotless again like we hadn't just pigged out voraciously. There was nothing left to do except move to the living room and have out the talk Dad suddenly seemed so desperate to avoid.

I walked into the living room, or well, living area since the living room and dining room at the condo are one big open-concept room, with the kitchen just off to one side and the two bedrooms, two bathrooms and Dad's office through a doorway between the living and dining spaces and down a hallway. I snuggled up in my favorite spot on the long white, oddly angled but surprisingly comfortable interpretation of a sofa, pulling my legs up underneath me.

While Mom's house was a mix of plants, antiques and casualness, Dad's was definitely more showroom modern, with the air of an art gallery. Each non-window wall of the living and dining spaces had one massive painting, displayed with the artist's information and media used in a little tag next to it. There were also several marble and metal sculptures in the large room, seemingly tucked in corners but at the same time feeling very much on display. I waited, looking at the *Visions in Red* oil splatter painting that was above the entertainment center, while Dad stood for a moment between the living and dining space, staring into nowhere. Finally, he sighed and went over to the white, modernistic recliner opposite my couch and sat down. He leaned forward, putting his elbows on his knees and held his hands together, looking at me.

"Seventeen years, I knew this conversation was coming," he started. "You think I would have known what to say by now."

I could see he was tense. "Just start at the beginning, Dad."

He looked at me. I mean, really looked at me. As if he was trying to read my soul or something. Maybe he was. "OK, but first I want to say this." Dad slid to the edge of his chair, leaned forward and continued to look at me hard, as if he wanted to be sure I was seriously listening. I sat up straight to show him I was, and he nodded when saw that. "I have never lied to you, and I am not going to start now. Everything I am going to say is absolutely the truth. No one is crazy, no one needs meds. Your mother knows all of this and can confirm it. If you want to call her after we are done talking, you can. But let me talk all the way through first. Hear it all out, see it all out. Can you do that?"

OK, ominous start. But this was my father. My dad. Why would he have thought I would ever reconsider his sanity? Or think that he would lie to me? Only way out was through, I guessed. I nodded at him, showing I understood.

That wasn't enough. "AnnaBella, I can't take a head bob." Woah, full name. This was more serious than I thought. "I need you to expressly say it. You will stay here, you will hear it all out. Tell me you will believe me."

"Dad." I became as serious as he was. "I will always believe you. I will listen to what you have to say. Can I ask questions along the way?"

Dad seemed to consider that for a moment. "Yes, but not at first, OK? Let me get the basics out. I'll stop and do a Q and A when I feel like you need it, and it is appropriate. Fair deal?"

I started to nod, but Dad kinda cocked his head to the side slightly. "Yes, Dad," I said. "Fair deal."

Dad took a deep breath, blew it out, then took in another one and began speaking. "You know the basics of your conception, but not the details. You know it was a legal arrangement between your mother and I, rather than a one-night stand or any sort of romantic relationship. But there is far more to it than that. Your mother was an only child, sort of homely and plain in her own eyes. I disagree with her on that, as much as I disagree with you when you say that about yourself, but I digress. Her parents were poor, not that dirt poor of extreme need, but a working poor. The ones who make too much money to get any help from the government, but make too little to really get along without it. Those in the gap poor. Your mom had done fairly OK for herself in high school but wasn't outstanding gradewise. She never did much extracurricular because her parents couldn't afford it. So, when it came time to apply for college, she had lofty dreams but her family didn't really have enough to pay for it and she really wasn't the ideal type for any scholarships.

"Her parents, your grandparents, like any other loving parents, wanted to make it happen for her. So, they cashed in their meager retirements, double mortgaged the house, and basically pinched every penny until it screamed to pay her way through her Bachelor's degree. Your mom worked too. School full time and waitressing full time. She did very well in her pre-law classes considering the effort, but still was not anything considered special by others who didn't understand her struggles.

"Six months before her graduation from the pre-law Bachelor's degree program, your grandfather had a heart attack. Three days later, he died in the intensive care unit of the hospital. Your grandparents loved each other enormously. Your mom believes that when she found your grandmother dead in her sleep the very next morning that she either died of a broken heart or just chose to leave to be with him. I've never had the heart to tell her it was actually suicide because your grandmother couldn't handle the stress of the expensive medical bills and funeral costs your grandfather left behind. Instead, she foisted that pain, doubled, on your mother.

"As a mostly Catholic family, your mother had been to church occasionally and had a nominally religious upbringing. With all the pain of losing both of her parents at once, and the overwhelming financial burden of paying the medical bills, for two funerals, and the last semester of college on a waitress' salary, it was no wonder your mother went to the church. She was looking for salvation, or help at least, from her god. But no help came from that way. In her anger at feeling unheard, she went a different way. Your mother, in angst and desperation and pain, called on Satan to make a deal. And I answered."

Dad paused his story. He had not looked away from me as he talked, nor I away from him. But he waited here for me to react. At first, I didn't get it. He answered when Mom called. He answered when Mom called... on Satan. "Why would you answer when Mom called on Satan?" I didn't even realize I had said that question out loud until he responded.

"Bella..." He was speaking very softly, not quietly, but gently, like he was afraid his voice might break something. "Because I am Satan. Or at least something akin to that. Humans have a lot of this religion stuff messed up, and almost all of the stuff about a tempter or bad guy is wrong."

OK, now I could understand the crazy stuff in Dad's first bit. Yeah, OK. My brain was trying to process and it wasn't working out so well. Dad doesn't lie to me. Dad's not crazy. Dad said to hear him out.

DAD JUST FREAKING SAID HE WAS SATAN!! Dad is batshit bananas, y'all! Mom knows this? That Dad thinks he is Satan? And she just, what? Let me go with him! Is Mom crazy too? Or was that a lie? Does Mom even know…

"AnnaBella Cain." My dad said my name and my mind stopped short. My train of thought just floated away, kind of the same way the lies I would think to tell him did. "You promised to believe me. You promised to listen. Will you keep that promise? Even if you only believe right now in a 'for the sake of the conversation, let's assume it's true' kind of way, will you hold to your word?"

My brain wanted to run. I wanted to call Ricky the doorman up, the police, Child Protective Services, somebody. Hello? Yeah, my dad has snapped. He lost all the marbles there ever were. Come take me away to safety, please? But deep down somewhere in me, that promise was like a warm chocolate fudge on a cold ice cream sundae. Take it as truth. Hear him out, It told me softly. The more I quieted my brain, the stronger that feeling got. Trust him. Just for now, trust him. You can call CPS later.

OK, another interruption. Sorry. I promise not to make a habit of this, but I need something from you now. I need that same promise I made my dad from you. I know you are reading this and thinking, 'It's just a story. It's entertainment.' But I need you to promise me that, if for no other reason than the sake of conversation, you take everything you are reading as the truth. It may not match with your beliefs, or your ideas about how the world works. And that's OK. But the decision you need to make requires you to believe, even if only for now. Your brain is telling you, 'Say yeah but it is still just a story', but stop for a minute. You feel it? That tugging in your gut, in the core of who you are? That warm feeling resting right on top of the ice in the middle of your very identity, your most pure self? It's telling you to believe. Let go and let yourself feel it. Let it spread. And if you get to the end, make your choice and then forget that tugging was ever there, that's OK. Walk away, forget it ever happened, make it just a story for fun, that's really OK. But for now, promise me you will set aside what you thought you knew, what you thought you believed and take everything I say as the truth. I won't lie to you. I won't even embellish a little. I can't. They won't let me, even if I wanted to. For you, this is a moment in time, one little read, a quick decision and back to life as you knew it. For me, it is my life, all of it, for as long or short as you decide to make it. You promise? OK, good.

I could barely whisper. "I am holding to my word."

Dad waited a beat, then continued. "I have many names. Or at least there are many names people have called me throughout the millennia. Satan, the Devil, Ash-Shaytan, Belial. But also Yama, Osiris, Mara and many, many others. Some faiths do not have a name for me and what I do. Some believe Death itself does the job. Because each religion, each belief, has set itself up as the only real faith or at least the best faith, and each one only understands a fraction of the way it works, human ideas have become muddied and convoluted."

My face must have shown confusion, because Dad stopped speaking and took a breath. He shook his head slightly. "I am not doing this very well. Sorry Bella Bella." He got up from his chair and paced in front of the couch, back and forth a few times. My eyes never left him. I was either intrigued or terrified. I couldn't tell you then, and I can't tell you now, which. Probably both.

Finally, Dad stopped and looked at me again. "OK. So, here's how it is. All of the religions of the world, all of them, are right. And they are all wrong. All of them, the ones that died out thousands of years ago, the ones going on right now, and the ones that people will think up in another thousand years. The universe, the heavens, the everything that ever was or will be existed because of a power. This power. It created everything. It is not something that can be explained in a way that humans can understand. Even the gods don't understand It. We know It, we feel It, we are made of It but we have no idea what It is or how It works. Is It conscious? Does It make decisions and cause things to happen? No clue. Is It just raw power that happenstanced into creating life and the universe and the way of things? No idea. It does not follow the laws of nature, physics, miracles, nothing. There is no box you can put It into to even describe It. But from It, or by It, or because of It somehow, everything that ever was and ever will be exists. The gods, all of them, are made from It, or are imbued with It, contain It. Lots of It. When a human believes in something, some type of deity, truly really believes in that god, that god exists.

"We are not sure if gods come into being because the human believes in them or if the human believes in them because It made the god came into being. The two seem to work like a mobius strip, no beginning, no end, just an eternal loop with before also being after. There are gods that exist that no one has believed in since man lived in caves. There are gods that exist but man won't believe in them for another hundred thousand years. But these gods are the most It. They have, are made from, the most of that power.

"The rest of us, I guess most people would call us heavenly beings, have some. We are not as much of that power as the gods. We do not have the power to really interfere in human lives. We can do a little, more than humans give us credit for sometimes, and sometimes way less than they assume. The gods are the judges, the creators of the rules and laws. Some rules and laws the whole of all the gods agreed on together. Like the law of gravity, that's a joint commission thing. Individual gods can choose to cause a miracle here or there and do a one-off defying of the joint commission laws, but on the face of it, no one god has the power to outright change those rules by themselves.

"Each god, or group of gods if they decided to tag team together, gets to set the rules for their worshippers. These are like the ten commandments type stuff. The way humans who really believe in them should act. They also get to set up any reward or punishment system for their believers that they want, too. Heaven, hell, purgatory, Valhalla, reincarnation in varying shapes and sizes. To each their own.

"Humans have a very, very tiny bit of It, that power. Just enough to send them searching for more of It. Some animals do too, but those are few and far between. Most animals have just the tiniest dab that makes them alive. But humans have enough of It to make them crave more. Hence, why humans seek out faith and religions and stuff and commit themselves to the rules the god of their choice gives them. They want that reward, which usually involves getting to a place that they can bask in It, the power, full on."

Dad stopped speaking for a moment. He let me absorb all he said, and then asked, "Need a drink? I need a drink, let's take a break and grab a drink."

I didn't speak or move. I wasn't confused, and I was way past whether or not I believed. I was trying to wrap my head around something bigger than the existence of a god. That the gods were created by something so much bigger that even they didn't understand It. Kind of like how we can't really understand the gods. This was a little difficult to really grasp for me. I had always functioned under the idea that there was something bigger, more, some sort of ultimate being, but never really considered it in any concrete way. I never had really thought of it as a god, or multiple gods, or whatever. So, to try to all at once make my sort of translucent ideas about a higher being into something solid, while also accepting that this higher being was not the highest being but some sort of creation by an even more unknowable force, was hard. It was like cornstarch and water, liquid when it moved, solid when you poked it, but slid through your fingers like quicksand.

Dad had walked away to the kitchen and came back with a cherry cola for me and something in a small glass with ice for him. It looked like alcohol. He handed me my cola and took a big swig of his drink. He sat back in his recliner again, leaning back and sipping his drink. He waited until I had composed myself enough to open the cola bottle and take a sip.

"You good?" he asked. I nodded in response. "Questions so far?" he pushed.

I thought for a minute, found my voice, which had mysteriously vanished, and asked, "You said the heavenly beings, um, you, are well, kinda in between the gods and humans, right?" Dad gestured with his hand that I was correct and to continue. "So, then what are they... you? Like angels and demons and stuff?"

Dad chuckled. "Well, kind of. The concept of angels and demons make it easier for people to understand. But there is no good side, bad side like most people think. All of us in-between beings, are just that. The in-between beings. Gods will go to humans themselves sometimes and do stuff, or bring humans to them, but that usually makes a mess. It really can screw stuff up, honestly, but who am I to tell my bosses what to do?" Dad chuckled again and I smiled. I didn't quite get the joke there but he was relaxing, so maybe I could too. "The in-between guys like me have jobs to do. Pretty specific ones. The gods kind of get free run of the joint, with only one or two really specific tasks they must do because they are setting up and running the faiths their individual believers are following. But for the most part, other than that stuff and the joint commission obligations, they do whatever they want.

"The in-betweens? We have one very specific task, and that task is our whole reason for being. We are not good, nor bad. We are neutral, only completing our assigned job. Some in-betweeners work for one specific god or god group. Like the Valkyries. They work for the Norse gods. Others, like me, have a job that is done for the whole of humanity and the full joint commission. Us joint commission guys are what usually gum up the works between one belief system and another because trying to explain something everyone has while maintaining your 'one true religion' status is messy.

"Especially when some people try to make my job evil. I am not evil, by the way. In my, I guess you could call it heavenly, form I am purely the job I do. I have no other identity than that. But the gods and the in-betweens sometimes get to come to earth and take on human form. It's good for us to do that every once in a while, so we stay connected, and understanding, to the human condition and do our jobs better."

"What is your job if you are not the bad oogie boogie you're made out to be?" I asked.

Dad contemplated whether he would answer that for a moment and finally decided not to. "Let's leave that answer for tomorrow when I take you to work, OK? There is a lot going on in that head already and I still haven't told you about Mom and me really yet."

He was right. My brain was already almost mush. "Then tell me about Mom and you," I pushed him.

Dad leaned forward again, saying, "OK, a tiny bit more back story, then Mom and me." He was smiling now a lot more. I wasn't sure if it was that I was still listening, and at least on the face of it accepting what he was saying, or if it was that the drink was alcohol and he was just getting buzzed. "In the beginning," Dad chuckled at this turn of phrase, and had to start over. "Ahem, in the beginning, they all made a lot of mistakes. The gods, the in-between guys, all of them. They came to earth a lot. A lot of them got comfortable and made real lives here. And had an uber crap ton of kids here, with humans. I mean, for real, Zeus? He had so many he could populate Greece with them. Oh wait, he kinda did…"

Dad waited a beat, saw I was unimpressed by his joke and moved on. "Anyway… A lot of those kids ended up quite messed up. We didn't understand how that power, It, worked and how the heavenly It would combine genetically with human It. Or in some cases, would refuse to combine. We actually still don't quite understand it, but that's beside the point. A lot of stuff went screwy, and a bunch of half heavenly, half human kids went clinically insane. The commission came together and basically said, 'Enough of that', sent a flood, wiped out the crazy ones, and put in a joint order that no one could make any more part human kids without permission from the board.

"The board didn't give permission often, but you have heard of one case, of course. That dude in Israel two thousand years ago? Yeah. But in either case, this led to rumors and stuff among the humans about having babies with the gods or angels, and of course, century after century those stories mutated. Eventually, there came a rumor that if you asked the right way, you could give a god or angel or demon your kid and they would grant you favors. You could sacrifice your first born to them for stuff.

"Anyway, so my job when all this was going down was pretty relentless. I never got the chance to come here and make a family like all the other guys. Honestly makes me wonder how my name got tied up with the whole sacrifice your kid for power thing, but there it was. Everyone else at work had at least one offspring that had genetically inherited enough of It to become at least a demi-god or an in-betweener. So, they all had help with their day-to-day operations. But me? I was slogging away at one of the most difficult positions with no time to make a family. One day, though, I decided enough was enough and I wanted what everyone else had. So, I approached the commission and asked if I could take some time, telecommute for work and be down here for this stuff. They agreed.

"Wouldn't you know it? I get down here and the first thing I hear is someone calling out for me. They never call out for me unless they want to do something shady, but this one didn't want that. It was your mom, and she just wanted the pain gone from losing her parents. Or if not that, at least a little help to get out from under the crippling debt and maybe a financial stream to pay for law school. She would work for everything else on her own, she just wanted tuition. She intrigued me, so I stopped by.

"Scared the ever-loving piss outta her when I showed up, truth be told. She didn't think she would get an answer. But we talked. I calmed her fears about the 'sacrifice your first-born rumor', but told her I was interested in having a kid. Like no, really, I want to be a dad, so maybe a deal could be reached, if she wanted to be a mom. If not, maybe I could find another way to help her. But your mom wanted a child too, but didn't have the resources or time for a relationship or the money to provide the type of life she wanted to give her child. A life that was financially easier than what she had growing up. When I told her we could come to an agreement to give her all of those things, and the child to go with it, as long as I was part of that child's life too, she agreed to discuss it with me.

"After months of talking, negotiating, and whatnot, we came to an arrangement. I took care of all her financial debts, gave her a significant lifeline of cash to get through law school, plus living expenses. She was killing herself trying to do it all, and it was stupid for her to continue that when I basically could just print money. I threw in as a freebie some updates on her looks, not because she needed them, only because she wanted them but wouldn't ask. It helped her feel more self-confident and to have a backbone. I may have also given her a little push with those too. I wanted the mother of my child to be proud of themselves and teach my kid to not take no gruff. She didn't need an upgrade to her intelligence or ability to do well as a lawyer. The way she haggled custody of you with me? She didn't need that by a long shot.

"I couldn't do anything for the pain of the losses in her life as a heavenly being, but I did as much as any friend could. I listened, and I think that helped her a lot. And the rest? Well, the rest is pretty much what you know. After she finished law school and got that awesome job, all by herself by the way, no push or help from me, we went down to the clinic, and did all the stuff to make you. You were implanted in your mom while I was at work in the, for lack of a better word, heavens. I came down for all the important stuff and if you or she ever needed anything, and since you were born, I have worked from here, commuting to work when I am not with you."

My mind had started wheeling around again and Dad could tell. He went to the kitchen, refreshed his drink and came back out, this time choosing to stay standing. He leaned one shoulder against the entertainment center, glass and chrome of course, crossing his feet at his ankles. He looked for all the world like he was just discussing the last World Series game instead of the root of all faiths in humanity and his decision to make a half-human, half-angelic baby with a woman he hardly knew.

"You have questions. Ask away," he told me, taking another drink.

"What about all that stuff with Mom on the porch?" I started. "What about my seventeenth summer being important? And what tests? And what's up with my eyes?" I was having a hard time focusing on so much information. I really had a million questions about how Dad heard Mom and knew what she wanted, how he did that stuff to help her. Where did his money come from if he worked for heaven? Why did the gods each decide to make their religions the way they did with so many of them being mean to other religions or even their own people? What was his job then really and how did it keep him so busy in those early years? And on and on. I stuck to the ones that seemed easier, the ones that could tell me where I fit into all this.

"The human-heavenly hybrid children are, for the most part, normal growing up," he explained. "There can be signs of an over-human amount of It in them as they grow, but usually It comes out in harmless ways. Like someone having eye colors that just won't pick one and stay that. Or eye color that changes when people around them lie, or they get angry, or stuff like that. Sound familiar?"

It did. I didn't need to tell him it did. I had remarked on my weird eyes a lot growing up. So, he just kept talking. "The problem comes when the children become adults. Interestingly, adulthood is set by societal standards and isn't a concrete thing. In our society, adulthood is usually considered to start at eighteen years old. So, I needed this summer to check if you have It, how much It you have, and if there was too much It to be safe. I'm pretty comfortable with that last part. Most kids with way too much It to be safe start showing signs of severe mental instability years before now. You've got a pretty clear account there, so I think we are good. But did you inherit only a little extra and are basically just a gifted human? Or is there enough for you to really come work with me, to be one of the in-betweeners? This I need to check."

I sat for a while, not knowing how to say what I really wanted to say. The thing we all would really want to ask for at a moment like this. I wanted to believe my dad. I had promised. The warmth over cold was still there. But somehow, I needed... 'Proof'. I finally just said it.

"You want proof." Dad did not ask me, but made a statement. "OK, I can understand that."

Dad stood up straight again and set down his drink on the entertainment center. He stood up tall, somehow becoming taller than I have ever seen him before. Slowly, so slowly that at first I thought my eyes were tricking me, he started to glow. Not this external glow like you see angels on TV do. Not the halo around the head glow like they paint stuff in art, like on the Sistine Chapel. But an inside of him glow. Like a glowstick you get at concerts. The ones that look plain then you snap them and they emit a soft sort of light that doesn't go out away from them, but just hovers there, right below their surface. A glow that would probably be invisible to the naked eye in bright daylight. It started in his middle, and just expanded throughout him. I could still see all of his features. He was still my dad, just the glowstick version.

The more he glowed, the stranger I began to feel. At first, it was a little tickle. The sensation was like static electricity from rubbing wool socks on carpet racing up and down my arms. Then I couldn't hold still. I had to stand. I did and began to walk towards my dad. The closer I got the stronger I felt it, the compulsion to tell him everything. That time I tried a cigarette and Mom grounded me but didn't tell Dad because she said me throwing up and losing my phone for a week was punishment enough. The time when I was three and peed the bed because, yes, three glasses of water before bedtime was too much.

I was halfway to my father when the sensation changed. It changed so fast that the room spun around me. It went from tingly and pushing me to pulling out of me and hot, no... ice, no... hot. The living room faded away. My dad disappeared and before me was a nothingness so deep, so vivid, so tangible that all of the sensations I had ever felt went away. There was no sound, but it was extremely loud at the same time. The silence made me feel as if my ears were bleeding. I couldn't see anything at all except a black emptiness, but at the same time I felt as if I could see whole galaxies be born, grow and die around me. And the pulling sensation was still there, my insides trying to force their way out through each small pore in my skin. I was rushing everywhere but not moving. I was standing completely still and could feel the hair on my head and my eyelashes growing.

Then I heard my dad's voice again. "Fuck! Bella! AnnaBella! ANNABELLA CAIN! Focus on me. C'mon, focus. You can do it." My dad's face swam back into focus slowly, blurry at first then slowly getting clearer. "There you go, baby girl. There you are. Just breathe sweetie, just breathe. Holy spit fire and damnation, Bella." I was sitting on the floor, but I didn't remember sitting down. My body felt heavy and tired, but it was all there, inside my skin where it belonged. I looked at my dad and he was just my dad. Not glowstick Dad any more. But I could still see a little glowing and couldn't figure out where it was coming from.

"Who's glowing if you aren't, Daddy?" I asked. I hadn't called him Daddy since the fourth grade but somehow I felt like I was small again. So little next to those galaxies that had been in my mind, I felt like I wanted to curl into my dad's arms and hide, like I did after a bad dream.

Dad smiled tightly. "You are Bella. Let it go now. Just slow breaths, there's a girl, that's the way. Let it go. Good." I breathed slowly and purposefully the way my dad was breathing, copying him. The heavy, tired feeling slowly went away and apparently, the glowing went away with it because Dad relaxed a whole bunch.

"I glowed?" I asked again, still feeling like a small fourth grader.

Dad smiled gently. "Yeah, baby, you did." He pulled me up gently so I was sitting properly and then asked, "Do you think you are ready to move to the couch?" I nodded and he helped me move to the sofa. I had felt like I had walked a million miles away from that couch, but in fact, it was only a foot or two from me. Dad handed me my cola, and commanded me to drink. I did, and the sugary sweetness helped more of the smallness, and tired heaviness, fade.

We sat in the quiet for what felt like a long time, hours of just sitting, sipping our drinks. But again, time does not work like science thinks it does so I don't know how long we sat there. It may have only been a few minutes. When I finally felt like myself again, I turned to my dad and asked, "What about the tests? You were talking to Mom about that you would test me and make sure it was safe. Did you mean you would test the power It or something else, some other it? What did Mom want you to make sure was safe?"

Dad laughed and said, "This concludes the testing portion of our evening. You got It, the power It, and quite a bit of It." It didn't escape me that he never answered the second half of my questions, about what Mom wanted to make sure was safe. Oh well, later I guess. I had another question now.

"If you are really Satan, but Satan isn't Satan, what is your name? Because I am pretty sure a heavenly being with the power of It inside them is not named Nick Cain," I asked.

"Those are not my names, you're right," my father started slowly. He sat, thinking, then replied, "I have never had a name. We in-betweeners created by the It power aren't given them. We acquire names when we take a human form. Humans create names for us based on the interactions we have with them but they are not our actual name. Our corporeal form, and its accompanying name, are kind of a manifestation of both our jobs and the human concept of us. But they are not really a true name, per se. I think the only real name anyone has ever called me, the only name that was really who I am, was Dad."

I didn't know how to respond to that, so I didn't. Instead, Dad curled up next to me on the couch and held me like I was that little girl who had a bad dream again. Eventually we both seemed to come to an unspoken agreement that there had been enough discussion of the heavenly, or whatever it really is called, for one night and Dad handed me the TV remote. I turned on the TV and randomly flipped through the stations until I found a brainless show we could watch without having to do any hardcore thinking.

The rest of that night, Dad and I just relaxed. We watched dumb movies and ate popcorn and all around did nothing brain taxing. I think he knew my mind was overflowing, so he just let it all sift around in there and didn't add anything to it. Eventually, I went to bed. I don't think I even told Dad that was where I was going or said goodnight or anything. I was just done, so I went to bed and turned myself off. I didn't dream, I don't even really remember sleeping. I got into bed, still in my clothes, pulled up the covers, and closed my eyes.

I opened them later and it was morning. I guess that was sleep. Or maybe, like when a computer has a huge software update, I turned off and back on again. Rebooted overnight. In the light of the morning, everything Dad had said the night before kind of made a weird sort of sense. It worked. The software update had processed and the hardware systems had accepted the updates.

Just like the computer, the login time after a reboot takes longer than usual. I, by habit, got up, showered, brushed my teeth and my hair, dressed and came to the dining table for breakfast. I didn't think about doing any of those things. I did them as if I was programmed to and was just following my programming. Dad must have been up for a while because there were doughnuts and coffee from the bakery down the street already waiting. I looked at him quizzically, as he sat in a suit and tie, reading the newspaper and sipping one of the coffees. I am not usually allowed junk food for breakfast. Get a healthy start to the day, you know, doughnuts are a snack for later. And coffee? I've had it but only when one or both of my parents knew I had pulled an all-nighter, exams or whatnot, and knew I needed the extra shot of caffeine. Dad must have figured that, after last night, I would need some pick-me-up juice today. He wasn't wrong.

"Sugar," Dad said, gesturing to the doughnuts. "You need sugar to process your thoughts. I swear junk food really does help people think better. Some scientist should do a study on it or something. Plus, tapping into It for the first time can expend a lot of energy, especially as hard core as you did. Your blood sugar is probably low."

I grabbed a cruller and a coffee, and Dad and I ate in silence. He must have been right about the sugar because the more I ate and drank, the more awake and rebooted I felt. Dad put down his paper, took his last swig of coffee and looked over at me.

"So," he said rubbing his hand together, "ready to go to the office?" I nodded yes. "OK, I thought we could walk instead of drive. One, parking is a nightmare. Two, it will give us time to go over ground rules and job descriptions. Sound OK?"

I swallowed my last bite of doughnut, washed it down with a gulp of coffee, and replied, "Sounds good to me. You're wearing a suit. Am I dressed OK?"

Dad looked at my outfit of a black T-shirt that had pretty flowers and fancy script writing in pink that said, 'whatever', plain blue jeans, no rips or holes in them, and my favorite Converse sneakers. He waved my question away. "You're going as a human guest. You look fine. Remember, today is not a work day for you, just a tour and introduction." Dad stopped speaking for a moment, contemplated something, then continued. "Actually, that's a ground rules thing I need to go over with you."

I sat up straighter to show Dad I was paying attention. He did as well, I think making a physical change to indicate him changing from 'dad mode' to 'boss mode'. It dawned on me that I would have to figure out navigating Dad as boss, but all in good time, right?

When he spoke again, Dad's voice even took on a different tone. Not quite the seriousness that he had last night, but he definitely wasn't so easy breezy either.

"Couple of things. One, when we get to the office, don't call me Dad. Mr Cain is fine, Nick is OK too, but you are probably better off sticking with sir or just nothing. Even when you think we are alone. And for the love of everything, don't slip up and call me Dad."

Strange, but office etiquette was new to me so I figured maybe that's the way it was at all hoity toity law firm jobs. "OK, Daaa... Mr Cain." Well, that felt weird.

"Good girl," Dad replied. "In fact, rule two, try not to speak. You will have questions I am sure, but we can talk at home about them. You should have the air of some low It level human who is all shocked and amazed at this stuff. I mean, it probably will be incredible on some level for you, but the amount of It you have will probably buffer your jaw-slack, inability to process what you are seeing. But other people at work do not need to know or sense how much It you have. If they do, they will have questions for you, questions we are not ready to answer. So, act the way you think someone who only knew me as Satan and won a free trip to the heavenly lands would. Someone who did not get the conversation and explanations you got last night would. Got it?"

I nodded that I understood but part of me was starting to wonder if Dad wanted to hide the fact that I was his daughter from the other people at work.

"Good," he continued. "Third thing. Do not, I repeat, do not interfere. Most of the people I work with have humanoid type visages, but not all. You are going to see some freaky things. You might see things that look horrible or awful. You might see things happening to others who seem human that looks like they are being tortured or abused.

"I want you to remember this. Not everyone who looks human is. And anyone who is human is dead, besides you. What looks to you like pain may actually be pleasure. What looks like it is happening very fast may in fact be happening very slowly, or vice versa. Oh, and that reminds me of another point. Time is not what you think it is there. Time is kind of a human concept. It is not a joint commission law, but just a weird coincidence that works the same way some of the time, in some of the places. It is... well, it's hard to explain."

I waved my hand at Dad. "Sir, remember? I am a High. School. Student." I put a lot of emphasis on the words high school. "I have taken math tests in the very recent past. I know time is wack."

Dad laughed at this. "Yeah, true. OK, so I need you to understand, with your kind of human, kind of not make-up, time may or may not work right for you there." Dad sat for a second, then spoke again, in a tone I can only describe as the 'dad about to give the birds and bees conversation' voice. "And a weird question. Are you on your period?"

I shook my head no. "Not due for another two weeks."

"That makes things easier, OK." Dad breathed out. He continued, speaking normally, or well, normal but serious. "You may or may not feel the passing of time. You may or may not get hungry when you normally would. You may or may not get sleepy or have to use the bathroom. You may feel all the normal, human time passage stuff or none of them, or feel it sometimes but not others, or may feel one type but not another. It may come on suddenly or pass away suddenly."

Dad must have noticed my confused look, because he stopped speaking for a second, then resumed. "Let me explain it this way. It is possible you will be completely enjoying yourself, thinking you have been there only a short while, then suddenly have to pee like no one's business, like you haven't gone all day. Or find yourself starving like you haven't eaten in weeks. And you will feel like that because to your human body, you haven't. But because you have a little bit human, a little bit not going on, your body will work in fits and spurts. I am not human. I go to work and I lose all the normal humanness stuff. I never need to pee, or eat or sleep. If Mom goes to my work, she would feel the time normally, need to pee in what on earth would be two hours, get hungry at lunchtime, and need to sleep after sixteen hours or so.

"You are somewhere in between Mom and I, and how that will play out for you is very sporadic. So, if you need a human moment, you need a bathroom, or a sandwich or to call it a day and come home, tap me quietly on the shoulder. I will know that means you are asking for a break. I will try my best to remember to give you human moments, but like I said, I don't feel time there so I might mess it up. I am reliant on you telling me what you need and when."

OK, to sum up, I couldn't let anyone know I am his daughter. I couldn't let anyone know I am not strictly human. I was gonna see some weird stuff but have to ignore it. And I may or may not have basic human needs any more. I was not sure if this all made me more excited to go to work with Dad or terrified.

But Dad looked at his watch and got a surprised face. "Oops, running a little late. Ready to go?"

Time isn't real so how were we running late? Never mind, not important. "Yeah. Let's go. How far is it to walk?"

"Just downtown a bit, not far. It's a nice walk on a gorgeous day," Dad spoke as he and I got up and headed out the door. Once we were out of the condo, and he had locked up, he continued speaking while we went down the elevator and out onto the street. "You think of my job as if I am a prosecuting attorney and that is somewhat accurate. I do serve as the person charging people with crimes, but slightly differently than what happens in an American courtroom. Last night, I told you that all the different gods got to make up the rules their specific believers have to follow, and the punishments and rewards those believers get for following or not following the rules, right?"

I nodded, and Dad kept speaking. "Well, when a human dies, they have to account for their life. Did they follow the rules? How well? What should they get for their actions? Punishment or reward? The first thing that happens is another in-betweener evaluates the human's mind. They check to see what your real faith was. Not what you said you believed, but what you really, really believed deep down. Then a case is assigned to that belief system for trial."

"What happens if you didn't believe anything? Were atheist or agnostic?" I asked.

"Good question, Bella!" Dad exclaimed. "If you are agnostic, really agnostic and unsure of what was the right way, you are informed of the reality that every choice exists, given time to accept it, then have to choose which system of beliefs you would have chosen had you been sure in life. Now, you don't get to know all of them. You have to choose from the ones you knew while you were alive. Then everything proceeds as if you had been that your whole life. If you were atheist, staunchly atheist, a board of gods will be chosen for you. A lottery is performed where every existing god is put basically in a hat and a convention of seven gods are chosen to judge you on your life. Imagine thinking there is nothing after death and the gods aren't real and then ending up with a Venus statuette from the paleolithic era, Vishnu, and Zephyros the Greek god of the west winds judging your life. It's happened." Dad chuckled to himself.

I thought about this while we walked. Being judged by gods that no one has even worshipped for thousands of years? Is that really justice? Humans can only act on what they know and what they are given, so how does something that we only know of as a carving in a museum get a say in our eternity? I mean, humans are basically good, right? Besides those few nutzos, we may not be perfect but we try. We have free will, well I assumed free will still stood, it seemed like it, but we acted on our free will with no understanding of how this all works. So then how was this fair? Did fair come into it any more? Did it ever? Maybe not, otherwise why do kids get cancer? More questions for later, I guess.

Dad kept talking while I was thinking. "Instead of using their individual faith rules, the randomly assigned gods use a basic human decency chart that was created millions of years ago by the full joint commission and is updated every hundred years. (Oh, I thought, now that sounds more like a fair system.) Then, you get to choose one of the seven faiths represented on your convention as the punishment/reward system you get. You may be lucky and get a lot of reincarnation gods, so whether you are punished or rewarded isn't so bad either way. But if you end up with a lot of heaven-hell type systems on your convention, you may feel like a rock stuck in a hard place, because you have to choose your system before you know your verdict."

We had been walking straight down Waterburg Avenue, the street Dad's condo is on, this whole time. But now, instead of continuing straight towards the heart of the downtown district, Dad led us to the left, turning down Genoa Street. We crossed Waterburg and were walking past streets lined with pretty row houses. I knew this was an upscale neighborhood, and in a few more blocks we would enter a small shopping district that boasted nitchy stores that sold things like essential oils, crystals, home-made candles, and whatnot. I had never been past those stores on Genoa, but as we talked, Dad led us through that area and past it.

As we walked, he continued talking. "Now, there are obviously different rules for people who were forced to convert as adults. Or ones who were forced not to. They get judged by the religion of their hearts, not outward actions. And in cases of adults being sheltered too much to know anything else, who never had the option to know they could choose, like those born to cults or very isolated tribes, they are handled with special rules and usually only go before that god themselves in a closed session in the god's chambers. I don't work on those cases. I also don't work with children who died before they were old enough to really understand faith and choice and things like that. Those cases are in a whole other division."

The way Dad was talking about cases and dead children so casually made me look around. We were not the only ones walking down the street, as our city is planned so nicely, and it was such a wonderful day, that I think a lot of Thursday morning commuters had decided to walk or bike instead of drive. Better for the environment anyway. Dad noticed my surreptitious glances and laid a hand on my shoulder. "They can't hear us. Not really. Yes, they can see us. But remember, they don't care. To them, we are just another father and daughter on their way to wherever and our conversation is unimportant to them. So, it just slips in one ear and out the other. Unless we draw attention to ourselves, they probably won't even remember seeing us in five minutes."

I sighed some relief at this, and asked Dad, "What is it exactly that you do, then? People die, they are evaluated to determine what they really believed when they were alive, and then what? There is a court case to see if they followed those rules?"

"Exactly," Dad said. "The rules of their religion, their faith, whatever, and their faith only, are used to judge the actions of both their hearts, their minds, and their bodies for their whole life, starting at when they accepted that belief. Some people knew from the start what they believed. Some people changed along the way and their actions changed once they found their true calling. Some people screw up a lot before they find faith, and as a courteous gesture, the gods ignore behaviors that happened before really accepting that belief. Like you wouldn't punish a kid for doing something wrong when they are too young to understand, we do the same with adults and faith. My job is the prosecutor.

"In the courtroom for the judgement, there are three to four groups: me as the prosecution; the god or gods who run your faith act as the judge; and the person on trial defending themselves as decent and deserving of the reward. Sometimes, depending on the faith, the person on trial has a defense lawyer. Some religions have that, some don't. Christianity does. They believe Jesus died for their sins, so he acts as a defense lawyer for his people. Sometimes, the religion believes that there is only one being that represents good and bad. In those cases, I am both the defense and the prosecution. But for the most part, I am the prosecution. I tell the judges the offenses, the bad stuff, the rule breaking stuff the person did and they have to defend themselves as to why it shouldn't be held against them or that the good stuff outweighed the bad.

"Then the gods judge the testimonies given and decide if the person should be rewarded or punished, or if their religion has it, given a third option in between. I have no stake in the outcome. I don't necessarily want people punished. It is just my job to make sure the gods have a fair and accurate account of each person's life. Honestly, my favorite cases are the ones where I get to say, 'Your Honor, except for a small bit of expected juvenile delinquency and minor human errors quickly corrected, this person has followed the rules well. I have no case to put before you and move for a summary reward finding.' Those are the best cases, but they don't happen often."

While I sorted all this out in my mind, we walked through the Genoa Street shopping district. A few blocks past it, Dad indicated for us to turn left again, cross Genoa and continue on down A Block Row. I had never been down this street and as we walked and talked, the buildings changed from being single homes to squat, one- or two-story nondescript brick buildings. Most of them didn't have signs to indicate what they were, but just address numbers or descriptors, signs saying 'Building A2' or whatever, like you would see in a medical park.

"What happens if someone misunderstood the rules?" I asked. "Like really misunderstood them and did something wrong because they misunderstood?"

Dad got a huge smile. "Bella, my beautiful, smart girl!" he exclaimed. "Look at you, figuring out the important stuff. In a case like that, we sidebar. The examiner is brought back in and some questions are asked. First, why did the person misunderstand the rules. If it was not their misunderstanding, if a human a long time ago changed how the people of that faith understood the rules, or parts of the rules were lost, they get a reprieve. This happens. Writing history is the right of the conqueror. Records are destroyed. Or things happened so long ago that no one knows. Like the Nicaean Councils, or the burning of the Library of Alexandria, or the writing of the Talmud. In this case, the person is not found to be at fault for their actions and is judged on the rules as they knew them.

"If, in other cases, they should have known or had every opportunity to learn the real rules, no dice. They are judged on the rules as they are, not as they thought they should be. This one is happening a lot lately. Christians actions being based on Leviticus when it suits them, but then saying they have been freed from Old Testament laws when it doesn't. People who take on the beliefs of Buddhism, but only following the basic ideas you get from a Google search, and never researching the real stuff. People who pick and choose pieces of this religion and that one, this urban folklore and that, smushing them together and calling themselves Wiccan or Pagan or some such other very real religion with a real set of rules they could have learned and followed properly had they actually tried.

"If they really believed themselves to be something, and really believed they would be deserving of the rewards of that faith when they died but made no real effort to learn how that faith actually works and what the true rules they had to follow to get that reward was, then, well, that's it. They are held accountable for their failure to really follow the rules they ascribed themselves to and get no leniency."

Dad must have seen a ton of other questions brewing in my mind. He stopped walking and put a hand out to stop me. "Listen, Bella. If you choose someday to follow me into this job, all the ins and outs will be explained. You don't need to get it all now. For today, just understand that every person who comes into my courtroom signed up for their judgement in the exact way it happens for them. We, the gods, the defense, me, we all will be fair to a level the human courts could never be. We physically cannot change the rules or let any personal bias get in the way. We don't have personal biases because we are not people. This is it."

At first, I thought Dad said the it with the capital I, the power It. But then I saw him point to a small building and knew he meant we had arrived at his work. The building looked very unimpressive. It was only one story, brick like the rest of the buildings around it. There was no parking lot in front or walking path up to the front door. The well-kept grass just grew right up to the door, a basic glass office door with a handle that said 'Push' on it. There was no identifier on this building, no number, and I noticed no mailbox. If we hadn't have stopped here, if Dad hadn't have pointed it out, I think I would have missed that the building was there all along.

It wasn't invisible. While we stood there, a man walking towards us with his dog saw and felt it. His dog wandered on to the grass to do its business and the man took the opportunity to lean against the building and pull a stone out of his shoe. Then he bagged up the poo and kept walking.

Dad looked at me again. "Remember time is not an exact science, space isn't either, nor distance. Take my hand, Bella." I took Dad's hand, and without having moved, we were standing in front of the door, close enough to touch it. Dad waved a tan plastic badge he materialized from one of his pockets over the door, pulled it open, and still holding my hand, we walked through together.

Inside the door, the foyer of the building seemed to go on for miles. The walls were a slight golden yellow color that was both pleasant but seemed opulent at the same time. The floor was a plush purple carpet. There was a huge water fountain in front of me, made of marble, depicting what at first looked like a woman and man dancing. But the man and woman seemed to shift as I looked at it and they began fighting, then were holding each. The statue had to be at least three stories tall. As my eye looked up at the statue, it continued to follow the rest of the building up... and up... and up. A hundred stories, maybe more.

I turned around and looked back out the glass door. Outside was not A Block Row any more, but a bustling street in a huge city. The city was not my city, I knew that. Nobody made skyscrapers out of gold. I could tell they weren't just painted gold, but really were gold. And the streets were made of brick pavers, except they weren't the normal red or brown brick but glass. The sunshine reflected on them, causing prisms of rainbows to spill into the air everywhere. And there were people, lots and lots of people, like New York City busy people.

The people were all sorts of colors. Some of the people looked human, white, black, brown skin and hair and eyes, with two arms and legs, one head. They were as normal as anybody you find on a Sunday bus. Others were not so normal. One guy, I think it was a guy, was green, like lime green, with orangey-brown stripes on his face and he had three legs. Another, gender very unspecific, had two heads. One head was a lion and the two heads seemed to be talking to each other. The lion head looked mad at what the human head was saying and it seemed like they started to argue as they moved out of my view.

I pushed the building door open and looked through the empty space past the doorway. The actual empty space. There was nothing there. Not A Block, not the street of glass, nothing. I turned to Dad, my face showing all the confusion and he just waved the badge at me. Oh. I hadn't told the door where I wanted to go. So, it went nowhere.

Dad took my hand again and started walking away from the door deeper into the building. I followed, looking around as I went. There was what I assumed to be a reception desk on my right. Behind it was a bank of offices with glass walls and doors. Some of the offices had the blinds over their glass walls closed, but others had them open and I could see just as many varieties of beings in the offices as were on the glass street.

I looked to the left and there were a bunch of temporary wall dividers. It looked just like any other regular office building with cubicles making up tiny office spaces for those workers not high enough on the roster to warrant a real office. I couldn't see very well into the cubicles, but heard many different languages, or at least I assumed the noise was all talking, coming from them. I heard English, French, German and Spanish, and some languages that I could only guess at. But some of the noises sounded like there was no way a human throat could make them. As I glanced around the cubicles, I noticed a man was on fire. Like, all the way on fire, flames from his feet to well past his head. He was screaming as he walked between the cubicles and into the foyer area.

I made a noise in my throat. Surprise and fear jumped out of me and I lurched against Dad's hand. Shouldn't somebody be doing something?

Dad pulled me back towards him and whispered in my ear, "Remember the rules?" Oh, yeah. Then louder, he said, "That's just Bob from accounting. He's like that until he has his first cup of coffee. Hey, Bob!" Dad waved with his free hand. Bob waved back but kept walking, screaming and burning.

We came to a bank of elevators, one of which's doors were standing open. We got inside it and the bank of buttons said there were four hundred and seventy-three options. I would say floors, but my mind was settling into the idea it probably wasn't that simple here. Dad pushed the button for three-three-three, and the doors closed. The elevator moved, well, like an elevator feels like it moves normally and after a moment, the doors opened and a robotic voice said, "Three-three-three, going up."

When the elevator stopped at three-three-three, Dad and I got out. We walked out into a room that could have been any office anywhere, except it was busy. To the left was a waiting area. It had those normal, waiting area at a doctor's office plastic and wood chairs. But a lot of them. I tried to count but there were so many. Probably five hundred or so. The chairs were full and some people had to stand.

All of the people in the waiting area looked like normal people. A sea of all types of people, but regular people nonetheless. Some of them were crying, some crying hard. Others seemed to be smiling and very happy. But most were just waiting, that impatient look on their faces like what you get when your appointment was at three and it was now fifteen after and you just wanted to get this over with already.

In front of us was a desk, with a young man sitting at it. The man also looked normal, and busy. He was white, well rather pinkish, but the normal pinkish a Caucasian person turns when they get just a little bit of a sunburn, and had blond hair, shaped in a crew cut. He didn't seem very tall, but the desk cut him off at the waist. His top half at least was wearing a white dress shirt and blue tie, but the tie was pulled down, loosened from his neck. There was a dark blue suit jacket slung over the chair behind him and a few clipboards sat on the desk in front of him.

When Dad and I approached the desk, the man looked up. In a thick southern accent, he said, "Mike, glad you made it in finally." He noticed me and smiled. "Groupie today? Cool, anyhow, busy day. A flight from Shanghai to London, with a layover in Frankfurt went down. No survivors. All major branches on deck. Should I arrange for a brunch for your visitor?"

Dad smiled in a business professional sort of way. "Jim, yes. An extra viewer today. I did all the requisite paperwork for a full viewing, rather than the normal one for them. You should see that on the calendar." Jim typed on the computer, then nodded. He found the paperwork. Dad kept talking, "No brunch, I've arranged for snacks in the courtroom. Can you assure that Room thirteen is requisitioned as a necessary room in case human needs are required?"

At this, Dad turned to me. "Room thirteen is an all-purpose room that can be whatever we want it to be. It's down this hall." He pointed to a hallway to the right of us. "And on the left. It will be marked 'Ladies' Bathroom' when and if you need it. We don't need bathrooms normally."

Dad turned back to Jim and lowered his voice. "Has my request for access to Lot One been approved?"

Jim did not lower his voice. "Yes, but you were not given the full asking time. They only granted ten weeks from entry, not twelve."

"Shoot," Dad whispered, talking to himself. "I knew they would do that. No one gets twelve any more. Oh well, we'll make it work."

Jim held out a stack of files to Dad, who took them. "Starting in five," he said, and then went back to his ringing phone and computer.

Dad looked down at the files, and then at me. "Doing OK?" I nodded and he let go of my hand, and started walking down a hallway that wound to left and behind the front desk, flipping through the files as he walked. I followed him.

Down the hallway, there were only two doors. One, off to the left side, was wood and said, 'Courtroom'. One at the dead end of the hall was silver and said, 'Commission Room, Entry Forbidden Except Under Full Escort'. We went into the door on the left.

Inside this door was a room that for all the world appeared to be a regular courtroom, like you see on *Judge Judy* or something. Two large wooden tables sat on either side of the room with rolling office chairs placed behind them facing the front of the room. The big, tall desk in the center up front, sat higher than everything else, like where the judge would sit in a regular courtroom. Behind the judge's desk were a few stairs that led to a door. There was also a small desk to the right side of the judge's platform, lower than the judge's but higher than the two tables. The only things missing were the seats for people to watch from. There was one metal folding chair randomly stuck behind the left side table. I assumed that was for me when Dad went up to that table, put his files on it and sat down.

It seemed like he had forgotten I existed. This was new for me, to be forgotten about, but this was his job. I understood. I went and sat down in the chair I assumed was mine. Before I knew it, someone came in the door we had just came through and sat at the other, the defense's, table. He was an older, pudgy, white man with short, cropped hair that was obviously dyed black, short stubble on his face and a beer gut. He was wearing a disheveled suit, and was crying slightly. With him was a long-haired black man wearing rough, handmade clothing and leather sandals, who was whispering to the white man, and seemed to be trying to comfort him. They sat down and my father, the white man and the black man all looked straight ahead.

A very, very, very old man, short and stooped, with no hair, almost no teeth, skin that looked more gray than any other color, but who moved better than I expected him to, came to the desk to the side of the judge's and stood, saying clearly, "Adam Christopherson, Catholic." He must have been the examiner. The old man then sat down and the door behind the judge's desk opened. A man in a white robe with long gray hair and a long gray beard came out and sat at the judge's desk. He was glowing very faintly.

"Prosecution, any assertions?" the gray man asked, his voice raspy but powerful. He was obviously the god acting as the judge.

Dad talked, but it sounded nothing like him. He sounded robotic but musical at the same time. "Baptized as a baby, took first communion at twelve, considered other faiths at fourteen to sixteen years old, ceased communion at that time, took communion again at seventeen and a half and continued communion for the duration of his life, with no more than a three-week gap in between each event. Gave confession at least bi-yearly, with the last confession given at…" Dad flipped through some papers. "Last Easter."

The black guy spoke up. His voice was very melodic, and quite soothing. "Move to strike any offenses prior to Easter of this year."

The judge turned to Dad. "Any objections?"

"Yes," Dad replied. "For the sin of anger, only fourteen out of twenty Hail Marys completed."

The black guy and the white guy bent their heads together, conversing in whispers. The black guy looked up and spoke, "Petition for clemency. My client has the beginnings of dementia and asserts he forgot his count at the time."

Dad pulled a little black box out of his pocket, and pushed a button. In the middle of the room, a moving image appeared. It was the white man. I could hear him saying Hail Mary prayers as he fingered a rosary. There was another sound over his voice. It was also his own voice, his thoughts, saying, "One, two, skip a few, ninety-nine, one hundred. Just like kids." The video showed the man's thumb slide over a few beads of the rosary all at once.

The judge banged a gavel and the image disappeared. "Clemency denied," he asserted. He looked at Dad again. "Any other assertions past Easter?"

Dad flipped more pages in his file. "Half a dozen minor acts of anger, one major act of anger." The black man started to speak, but Dad raised a hand to stop him. "The prosecution will agree the major act was warranted at the time and defensible, therefore not in and of itself punishable, but no contrition was made for it later or for any of the minor acts."

The judge turned to the defense table. "Any counter-assertions?"

The black man nudged the white man, and spoke. I knew he was speaking French, I knew it, but I heard everything he said in English. "Deathbed appeal for forgiveness. I made a deathbed appeal for forgiveness on the plane."

Dad interrupted the man. "Under the 1776 Joint Commission Act of Forgiveness, Section 123-B, Foxhole appeals of forgiveness are inadmissible if appeals for removal to safety are used in conjunction."

The judge turned back again to the black man. "Was an appeal for removal to safety used?"

The black man conferred with the white man, then spoke. "Appeals for removal to safety was used prior to, not at the same time as, appeals for forgiveness."

Dad again flipped through his notes, "The time between change in appeals was less than thirty seconds, Your Honor."

"I am ready to rule," the judge said. "One hundred years' purgatory, then admittance to heaven. Each prayer for the dead said in your name credits six months' good behavior. A candle without the prayer will count the same as a prayer, but a prayer and candle together do not count double." The judge banged his gavel again. The black man left the room the way he came. The very, very old man took the white man, who was sobbing but trying not to, by the arm and led him out of a door that appeared on the right side of the courtroom. After they went through it, the door vanished again. Dad set that file aside in a new pile and picked up a different one.

As he opened the file, he leaned back and spoke to me without looking at me. "Make sense yet? Jesus did his job as defense lawyer for Mr Christopherson, telling him what to say and when to say it, or speaking on his behalf. I just told the stuff I knew that contradicted what Jesus was saying. The Catholic god ruled and the man will go to purgatory now."

It really did make sense. Dad wasn't bad or evil or a tempter. He hadn't made that man get angry or even urged him to. The man did it all by himself. Dad and Jesus just worked together to make sure the god applied the rules fairly to him.

OK, I know this has been a lot of talk, talk, talk. I promise it picks up really soon. I won't bore you with the whole two days of trials I witnessed. Suffice it to say, they all pretty much ran along those same lines. Sometimes the dead person had a helper like Jesus, sometimes they didn't. One time, Dad had to play both sides and the god and I listened to Dad arguing with himself for fifteen minutes. I did get hungry the first day, and Dad pulled a sandwich out of his coat pocket for me. I never got hungry the second day. I didn't get sleepy or have to use the restroom either day. The judge's bench expands when it needs to because there is a group of gods instead of just one. The gods took on a lot of different shapes and sizes and the desk just accommodated them. There was one god that looked like an elephant, and another that was blue with lots of arms.

After the waiting room was empty the first day, Dad and I went home and had dinner and acted normal and stuff. We walked back the second day and it was all the same, full waiting room, Jim, all of it the same. Just different people and gods and stories. If you are interested, because you are weird like that, you could petition your local god for the transcripts of the two days viewed by AnnaBella Cain. They may let you read it. But I would wait until all this hullabaloo has blown over. The gods aren't so happy right now. Make your choice first, then ask in like six months or so.

The end of the second day, Friday, after work, Dad and I walked back to the condo in silence. I was processing everything I had seen. It was actually kinda cool to know it worked like that. Humans get to choose what system fits them. There are rules, there are always rules, but each person gets to choose the rules that fit their identity. Almost eight billion people on the planet, it never sat right with me that people thought we all had to play the same exact game the same exact way. But we don't, and that kinda rocks.

Dad seemed to have a lot on his mind. When we got back to the condo, he was still quiet. He went into the kitchen and made lasagna for dinner. I flipped through the TV stations, watching nothing in particular and gave him his space.

When the food was done, we sat at the table to eat, and Dad finally spoke. "So?" he asked me.

"So," I responded. "Your job is cool, like really cool."

Dad seemed to get really happy when I said this. "Would you consider doing this job? Working with me? I mean, you would get your own courtroom, your own caseload and whatever."

I thought about this. "What education would I need? College or a trades school or something?"

"No, no, no," Dad laughed. "We would provide all the training you need. A lot of it would come through It, the power. You would just know most of the information you need. Those rules I can say, and the functions of each religion? I just know them without being taught. There is a test you would need to take before being allowed to become what we have coined as an in-betweener, but I've made arrangements for you to take that test if you choose the job."

"Would I have to choose now? Take the test now?" The thought of taking a test unprepared threw me, I'll admit. I was doing pretty well in school, but the good grades didn't just come to me like they did other people. I had to study at least a little before exams or whatever to get the best grade I could. "Wouldn't I finish high school first?"

Dad was still chuckling. "I forget how the human mind jumps to conclusions a lot and misses the obvious. First of all, yes. The plans for the test are set. You have until tomorrow morning to decide. Sorry for the short notice, but some things just have to be that way. But just because you pass the test does not automatically mean you must take the job. Free will is still a thing." That was nice to hear, at least.

Dad was still talking. "Second, there is no prep work you need to do, no education or studying. It's not a test like that. There are obstacles you would have to overcome to prove you can work with the It in your system to a high enough level to be an in-betweener and do the job. Some of the obstacles will make you use just the It, some of them will require you to think outside the box and use your surroundings in a way most humans wouldn't think to. I believe that will all come naturally to you.

"If it doesn't and you fail, no harm, no foul. You just go back to your human life as someone a little extra, a little gifted. But don't think about that. You won't fail." Easy for Dad to say I won't fail. I wished he hadn't brought up the ability to fail because now I was worried about that along with everything else, and how do you worry about how you will fail a test when you don't even know how that test works?

"And third, yes. Just like we discussed you would go back to high school in the fall and only work part-time as a co-op position," Dad told me, breaking my decent into paranoia over failure. "When you graduate high school, you will either become a full in-betweener like me, or a demi-in-betweener. Full timers live in the other place full time and just visit here. We can remove our human characteristics and be just our It-based selves there. We get to spend time on earth and as a human, but that isn't our home. It is rare for a kid of an in-betweener to qualify for full time. A god's kid? Yeah, happens all the time. In-betweeners, not sure it has happened yet, but there is a first time for everything.

Demis live here on earth and retain their human faces and needs. They travel to work the same way I have since you were born, the same way we did today. On earth, they are more human than anything, but over there they are the same as full timers. The only difference is that demis age, until they don't want to any more, then stop. We full timers who were created rather than born, don't get to pick the age we were created at. And demis lose some basic human functions. They can't get or cause a pregnancy unintentionally, they can't die, and they have some power to make humans forget them, or at least only vaguely remember the parts the demis want them to.

"You would live with Mom until graduation, still seeing me every other weekend and at work for half your school day. Then, after graduation, whatever the test said, whether demi or full timer, you would become that. Mom knows the basics of how it works and will support whatever career choices you and the test make. I would know and you would always be my kid, plus my co-worker."

Dad talking about me failing the test made me think of another question. One I really wasn't sure I wanted to ask, but I did anyway. "Dad, if I fail the test…"

Dad started to interrupt me, "You won't fail…" But I made him stop and listen.

"Dad, if I fail. If I do, would you have another child? Would you see me any more?" I looked down. The idea of being abandoned by him, the dad who had always been a constant source of support in my life, made me so scared I started trembling. I couldn't look at him. What if I suck and he got rid of me to try again to make a kid more like him?

"Never." Dad spoke with more force than I have ever heard him use before. Not in the courtroom, not ever anywhere. "I will never, ever abandon you. If you are human, and just human, guess what? I love you. If you are full time? I love you. Demi? I love you. Two-headed monkey? I love you. And no. Under no terms will I try again with another child. I got so lucky with you. You are amazing, and I accept you as you are, with the identity you choose, or were given by genetics. Nothing changes that.

"Plus, your mom was a once-in-an-even-my-lifetime, which is by the way, eternal, find. None of my co-workers got a human counterpart in raising kids that great. That understanding. Your mom doesn't want more kids and I wouldn't want kids with anyone other than your mom, so let that completely go right out of your head. You're it, kiddo. My life's work. And that work looks pretty damn good from here."

I believed him. I really did. And I knew he believed in me. I stopped shaking and was able to look at him again.

"I want the job, Dad," I told him. I was sure then. Like, ninety per cent sure, maybe eighty-five per cent at the least.

Dad smiled the biggest smile I have ever seen. His face looked like he would break out in song and dance, he was so happy. "All righty, Bella Bella. Then you need to rest up. It's been a long two days and the Trials are not easy. You need good sleep. Hold on." Dad went into the kitchen, fumbled around in there for a few minutes, banging this and clanging that. Then he came back out with a steaming mug of something. I could smell it as he walked it over to me. Sharp, pungent, and totally gross smelling. It was like someone had melted a candy cane into a pot of five-alarm chili. Ugh. He handed me the mug. "Drink." I really didn't want to. "One sip. For me, Bella Bella?" he begged.

I took one sip and then… I woke up in my room in the morning with birds chirping, the sun shining, and me feeling like I just slept the best sleep anyone ever slept, ever. And Dad was sitting next to my bed when I woke up, waiting for me.

"We don't have much time, Bella Bella. Up and dressed, let's go." As he spoke, he was pulling me up and out of bed. And that is how the race of the Trials began.

Part Two: The Trials of the Arena

Dad rushed me around getting ready. I wanted to choose my clothes carefully, but Dad was antsy, so I grabbed whatever I could find. A random T-shirt with a band on it, blue jeans and my trusty Converse shoes. As I brushed my hair back into a sloppy ponytail, I tried asking questions, like what in the heck had been in that mug last night. But each time I stopped to ask him something, he just kept saying, "No time for questions now. Later, I will answer them later."

We each grabbed a leftover doughnut on the way out the door and walked to his work building the same way we had on Thursday and Friday, but Dad was moving fast. So fast, I felt like I was jogging to keep up. I tried asking more questions, this time about the test, while we walked, but Dad waved them away, saying, "Don't worry, Bella Bella. It will all make sense. You'll see."

Finally, outside a candle shop on Genoa Street, I pulled Dad to a stop. "Wait," I panted. "Dad, Stop. First of all, whoa, let me catch my breath. Your legs are like twice as long as mine, I can't keep up. But more importantly, I have to ask you this. Please." Dad stopped and looked at me, obviously trying to hide his impatience. He was not doing a very good job of it. "You said the test would require me to use It. How? How do I use It? You never taught me how."

Dad sighed, and stepped back from me. He seemed to think for a moment before he spoke. "Remember when you fainted in the living room? I was using It to force you to come to me, to reveal your truths. On normal humans, the It through me works to make them admit what they have done wrong, but has no other effects. For you, It called to It. That's why you fainted. Your It, the It to compel me to come to you instead of the other way around, and my It basically fought each other for dominance. That's how I know how much It you have. It wasn't lesser that my It, the way a human or even the child of an in-betweener's should be. It didn't submit to me but stood toe to toe with mine. Your It actually won. That's why you glowed and I stopped glowing."

"But how does that help? How do I make my It work without passing out again or you challenging me?" I asked.

Dad looked at his watch. He seemed really concerned about how long this was all taking. A look flashed across his face, but then he forced it away, becoming the same patient man, if a little strained, I had always known him to be. He replied, "OK, really quick. Call It. Just feel for that stuff that you felt pushing out of you right before you lost consciousness."

I looked around. It was Saturday so no commuters, but there were shoppers this early. A few.

"Your glow won't be perceptible in this bright daylight. And if you go overboard, I will stop you," Dad told me. I raised an eyebrow at him. He had just said my It beat his It. How would he stop me? "Pain," Dad replied, reading my mind. "It's how I stopped you Wednesday night. I slapped you. I hated doing it, but you were going to burn yourself up or something if you kept on the way you were. This time I will be able to do it sooner because I won't be under your thrall, and won't need as much force. A pinch should do. But try to not need it. You just need to feel It, not be full of It, OK?"

I closed my eyes. I didn't know what I was supposed to do so I just stood there, catching my breath. As my breathing slowed, I realized that warm over cold sensation was still in the pit of my stomach. It was really, really slight. So slight I would have missed it had I not been looking for something weird or different in me. I made myself notice that feeling. When I did, the feeling got stronger. The feeling started to get very intense and I thought that, if I was doing what I thought I was doing, the feeling was too much, so I backed off from it a little. I thought about something else, a flower Mom was growing, her lilies. Tiny white flowers with only one petal, and large, broad, dark green leaves. The feeling faded, but when I acknowledged it again, it wanted to roar back up. In my head, I thought 'No, just a bit will do, thanks'.

"Open your eyes, Bella," Dad said. I complied and looked down. My abdomen was glowing. My arms glowed then didn't, then glowed then didn't, ever so faintly. "Nice control for a first attempt," Dad said appreciatively. "You got it. Now let it go."

I made myself think of the warm sunshine and being super-hot on the beach. The cold feeling under the warmth melted and the glow went away. I looked at Dad. He was shifting from one foot to the other, looking at his watch over and over again. He was getting restless in a way I hadn't seen before. I could tell he really wanted to go, like yesterday.

I took a breath and started walking again. Dad tried really hard to let me set the pace this time, but he was all antsy. Finally, we got to his office building and Dad pulled out his badge. Except the badge wasn't tan any more. It was green. He waved it in front of the door, took my hand, and pulled the door open.

Inside the door was not his office building. Of course. The key was different, so it went somewhere different. Through the door was someplace outside. We stepped through to a field, like the ones you see in movies when they want to show heaven or someplace really calm and peaceful. Tall grass swaying slightly in the breeze, the ground sloping slightly and dotted with yellow and white flowers with some trees far off in the distance. Small insects were buzzing around. A bee flew by us. Just inside the door there was a stand with a small plaque on it. It looked like those plaques you see at a museum that describe what is in the display case in front of you. The bronze plaque was engraved, saying:

This is Area One, the first area created for the gods. It is the most recognized version of what Humans call Heaven, but at no point in history were Humans allowed here on a permanent basis as a reward for any religious system. Area One is home to many facilities used by the Gods and Coordinators. To the left of this sign is the Singing Hills, where voice manipulations allow for anyone to reach any octave while singing in worshipping a deity. The Singing Hills are mostly a tourist attraction now. To the right of this sign is the Shed of Grievance. Here Gods and Coordinators would conduct trial runs of actions they wish to do on earth and test the outcomes. Many have come to use this shed as a place to work out frustrations, without actually causing direct harm to Humans. Directly in front is the Trials Arena. When Humans, Gods and Coordinators were allowed to mate, the Trials Arena was used to test the products of those matings for power, and the ability to join the ranks of God, Demi-God, or Coordinator. Mating with Humans is now outlawed and the Trials Arena may be reserved for training purposes only. Permanent residence of Area One is now banned for all Gods and Coordinators, per the Act of Separation, Statute 3-45, Section 5, Subsection R. Please feel free to use this area for vacation purposes, and entertainment of worshippers. Remember, it takes all of us to keep

Area One beautiful. Take only memories and leave only footprints, Enjoy!

I looked up from the sign and saw Dad was already walking straight ahead. To my left, I saw the land gradually start sloping up into gentle rolling hills. To the right, was a silver metal building with a bright red door. It was gleaming in the gentle sunshine. Straight ahead, where Dad was headed, was a wood barn. It had been painted green at one time but had obviously fallen into disrepair from lack of use. The paint was faded and the door was hanging crooked. I followed Dad, catching up with him at the door to the barn.

Dad opened the door and it creaked. A few dust motes fell slowly to the floor around us. Inside, it was dark. I could see sconces lining the walls but they had a film of dust on them that muted the light they gave off. Just inside the door was another bronze plaque on a stand. Dad ignored the plaque and walked over to the wall on the right side of the door. There were two slits in the wall there, one small one on top and one big one beneath it and a big, black button on the bottom. Dad was wiping dust from these. There was a spot on the wall below the big button that had obviously been cleared of dust before we got there, and that section of wood stood out, dark and gleaming, next to the grubby wall paneling that surrounded it. Dad pushed on the clean part of the wall and a small door about the size of a microwave popped open, showing a hidden panel. He opened a hidden panel beneath the button and started fiddling around inside the exposed area of wiring that had been behind it.

I looked around the rest of the barn. There were twelve doors, six on each side. There was one lighting sconce by each door. The doors all had writing on them that I couldn't quite make out. The red painting used to write on each door had faded until the letters were almost gone. The doors were wood, but covered with dust too and looked a grimy black. I turned back to the plaque and read it.

Welcome to the Trials Arena. This area boasts twelve tests of power and intelligence. Each test is unique, with its own rules and guidelines. To become a God, Demi-God, or Coordinator, you must pass all twelve, each in their allotted timeframes. The test as a whole must be completed in under twelve weeks. Once passed, the Arena will assign Coordinators their positions within the Pantheon. Feel free to return to the Arena for training or promotion points, if valid for your position. When ready to begin, place your bio-card in the small slot in the wall by the door and press the start button. Once started, the Arena cannot be exited until all twelve Trials have been completed or twelve weeks have passed. For individual test training, see the Department of Promotions for a test exemption. Your bio-card will pre-set the Arena to only open the doors of the tests you choose on the exemption form. Your results will print from the larger slot. Good luck!

There was a smaller golden plate added to the bottom of the plaque. It was obviously newer and had tiny screws affixing it to the original bronze plaque, saying:

Do not place your bio-card in the testing slot in the presence of Humans. The test doors may be opened for Human viewing, but the Trials Arena may not be activated for Human use or for testing of Gods or Coordinators in the presence of Humans. Reference: The Articles of Joint Commission, Section 528, Subsection 45, Paragraph A-21.

Dad had finished playing with things in the panel and slapped it shut. He turned to me, wiping grime off his hands. "Ready?" he started. He stopped, then started again. "Wait. A few things first. One, remember time is crap. Your humanness will try to interfere, don't let it. You can go forever in this place and never need to eat, sleep, pee, or have your period. Don't let your body talk you out of that fact.

"Two, use the power, use It. How It will work for you is different than how It worked for me, so I can't tell you how to use It exactly. But you get one time per room to call up stuff you don't have with It. So, take your time, look around and figure out everything you think you might need and get your supplies all at once.

If you miss something, you will have to do without It and use only what is available in the test.

"Three, there is a timer in each room. It will tell you how long you have left for that specific test. Once you start the timer, you cannot start the room over or leave it until the task is done or the timer runs out. There is a main timer in this room that lets you know how long you have left for the whole Trials test. Try not to focus too much on the timers, they are a distraction to push you to fail." Dad stopped and thought for a moment. "Yep, that's it. That's all I can tell you. Ready?"

I nodded. Oh well, no going back now, might as well just get on with it. Dad slid his badge, his bio-card I guess, in the small slot. There was a groan, then some rumbling. Through the open door I saw massive, interlocking metal slabs slide down over the building. They must have circled the whole building because you could hear the slam, slam, slam as each one hit the ground. Once the slamming metal slabs stopped, a timer appeared hovering in the middle of the room. It said: *12:00:00:00:00.0.* A loud beeping came from somewhere. It beeped ten times, then stopped. When the beeping stopped, a door directly to my right creaked open. Dad pointed to the door and mouthed 'Go!', so I walked through the door.

So that you can judge me fairly, you need to understand something. I did not know. I didn't know about the bio-cards. I didn't know that when Dad put his bio-card in, there was system that tied the test rooms to his exact genetic make-up. I didn't know that when I stepped into the room, with only half his genetic make-up, alarms triggered somewhere else, alerting those coordinators that the tests were being used by someone not Dad. I didn't know there was a special alarm triggered that recognized I was an offspring of Dad's and that he was using the tests on me. I didn't know we were breaking the rules. I thought he had a special dispensation. I really did. Remember, I can't lie. I physically can't. As I am writing all this, there is a Defender of Truth with her hand on my shoulder. A Defender of Truth forces all lies away from whoever they are touching. Any attempt to lie while they touch you will be met with force. It's not like Dad or me, who compels truth, making you want it, prefer it. They literally force you not to be able to lie, or even exaggerate. Watch, I'll show you. My hair is blo blo bla bla brown. My hair is brown! MY HAIR IS BROWN!! Jeez! Owww. OK, OK, it was just an example for the non-omniscient crowd. Wow, did she have to make it hurt that much? Yikes. See, I couldn't even type that my hair was blonde or black because it is brown. BROWN! Yeesh. I don't know how much Dad knew or didn't know about the alarms and what was going on outside the Trials Arena, or if he knew what would happen outside the arena before he did this. All I know is that my dad is my dad, I can't help who my father is. And my dad said for me to take this test to see how much I am like him and that I could work with him if I passed it. So, I took the test. Would you do differently if it was you? Would you ask your dad to show you papers of dispensation for your birth? No, I don't think so.

Inside the room, there was a small square of plush purple carpet visible, just inside the door. The rest of the room was completely dark. In front of the carpet was another bronze plaque, on the same basic stand, identical to the ones I had seen before. Next to the plaque was a timer that said, *1:00:00:00:00.0*, similar to the one outside. I looked at the timer for a minute. I counted it out. One week, zero days, zero hours, zero minutes, zero seconds. I must have only one week to complete this task. One week, I can't leave this room? Right, right. Time is flexible here, human needs don't apply. OK. I read the plaque.

Test One: Bring the hide to the door. Only the hide. Complications: No known weapons can pierce the hide. Time starts when you step off the starting square.

OK, sounds interesting. I had to see the room and what was wearing the hide to figure out what to do. Carefully, I stepped off the square.

The rest of the room lit up. I was in an arena like in ancient Greece. A gate at the other end of the arena floor rolled up. The biggest lion I had ever seen walked out the gate. It was mammoth. Just huge. And growling. There was some spittle hanging down from its mouth, which was open just enough to show me some crazy big, probably crazy sharp, incisors. The lion's fur was very wiry looking, but wasn't one distinct color. You know those cars painted special so their color changes with the light as you walk around them? Yeah, that was the lion's fur. And its paws! Good grief, one claw was probably the size of my head! I could feel the reverberations in the dirt floor every time the lion took a step. And it was stepping… towards me! Crap, what do I do? I need to get its hide, and only its hide. So, I gotta skin it. Wait, first, I gotta keep it from killing me before I decide what to do!

I looked around for some way to defend myself from a ginormous beast. The only thing I saw worth anything was the tiers of seating behind me. The square of carpet that was the starting line was still there, now in the center of the arena, but the door had vanished and the circular arena was all around me. The dirt center of the arena was walled in on all sides by stones stacked up and concreted together. Above the walls were row after row of tiered seating made out of the same concreted stones. In the center of the seating was an area that looked like a platform. From my classes on ancient Greece, I figured that's where the rich and famous, or politicians would sit to watch the games. The tiered seating was up high. Maybe if I climbed up the stone walls to the seating area, I could get higher than the lion could go. Or at least put some distance between us and slow it down. I ran to the wall opposite the approaching lion and jumped. Yeah, like that would work. The wall was more than twice my height. I needed rope or something.

I remembered what Dad said about using It to call for stuff I needed. But I could only do it once per test. I didn't want to waste It on rope then need It for something more important later. I needed to think. Think. Where's that freaking lion? Crap, closer, but it was only walking, plodding towards me. I have time but not much.

I looked around again. What could I do? There! A spot on the walls around the arena floor just to the left of me was bowed weirdly. Some of the stones jutted out. I could use that spot like the rock climbing walls at the mall. I darted over to it and reached up. I could just barely reach the lowest loose stone. I pulled on it a little before I trusted it. The stone held firm. I pulled myself up with that stone as hard as I could with one arm, and looked at the wall again. There! Another jutting stone. I used my free hand to reach for that stone. And swung. And missed. Grrr! I braced my feet on the wall, feeling the tiny bit of traction old Converse sneakers could give, and hoisted myself again. Got it! The stone in my second hand held as I let go of my first stone and scootched my feet a little further up the wall.

This was hard. Way harder than they make it look in movies. I was sweating hard. My bra felt all sticky and wet. This was not the time to realize I forgot deodorant this morning! Finally, I inched my feet up enough that I thought if I pushed my legs straight, I might just be able to reach the top of the wall.

I looked back at the lion. It was walking back and forth, each pace bringing it closer and closer to me. It was stalking me, I knew. OK, no time to guess. One, two three, push! I reached as far as I could and my fingers just grazed the top of the wall. I pushed my fingertips against the wall face, trying to get them closer, to get even a tiny grip on the top. Two of my nails ripped off and started bleeding. Behind me, the lion growled. Great, it could smell my blood now and thought I would make a fine lunch. I told myself not to think about it and keep trying. Push just a little more… Got it! Yes! My fingers grabbed the top of the wall and I lifted myself high enough to use the stones that had been my fingerholds as steps for my feet. I climbed up and dove over the edge.

And plopped down on the hard stone floor of the seating area. Ow. I hit with my hip first and sharp pains ran up and down my leg. The lion dove to the wall and growled loudly. His growl turned into a roar, and pain or no pain, I was up and running. I went to the top tier of the seating area and stopped, looking back down at the arena floor. The lion was pacing back and forth but not attempting to climb the wall.

Good, now I could sleep. No, think. Now I could think! I have to kill an animal who is impervious to weapons. What kills that isn't a weapon? Old age? I don't have that long. Plus, it is probably ageless. Wait.

When I babysat the neighbor's dog, the vet gave us a whole list of toxic plants that will make a dog sick. That was for dogs, but maybe some of them work on cats? A lion is just a really big cat, right? Lilies. We had to move Mom's lilies so the dog wouldn't eat them, because they were super toxic for dogs. So, what if I fed the lion a bunch of lilies?

Cats are smarter than dogs though. Dogs will eat anything. Cats, not so much. So how do I convince that big old kitty cat to eat a crap ton of dangerous stuff?

I was pacing as I thought all of this. One eye watched the lion the whole time. It seemed to be contemplating the wall where my blood dripped from my broken nails. The lion licked the wall then snuffed a little, and licked it again. Blood. Meat. Food. It was hungry and wanted food. Meat is food and meat has blood. OK, now we were getting somewhere. I needed the world's biggest, tastiest steak and a whole lot of lilies.

How much time did I have? I looked at the timer in the middle of the arena floor. It read, *3:6:45:15.9* and was counting down. What? You mean it had been almost four days already? How?

OK, time for the big guns. I needed the steak and the flowers. It was time to call on It. I looked for the ice and warm in my belly. Out of nowhere, a door plopped down in front of me. I must have watched *The Matrix* and *Monster's Inc* too many times. A door, my It came as a door. It wasn't a wooden door like the entrance to the test, but a heavy black door. It looked like it was made of solid granite. The door handle was white granite. Tentatively, I opened it. Inside the door was all darkness, except for one spotlight. The spotlight shone down on the most massive steak ever. This steak would have fed a family of four for days. There were flowers too. From my mom's love of all things growing, I knew they were peace lilies, the most toxic of the lily family. Strange. I was using something called peace to kill something. Oh well, I could think about the philosophical nature of that another time. Right now, I needed to get to work.

I pulled the flowers and steak out of the doorway. The door closed and popped out of existence. I instinctively started grinding the flower petals up in my hands. They were soft and wet, and the wetness from them started dripping down my arms. Not sure what part of the flower was the toxic part, I let the wet stuff drip all over the steak and kept grinding. When one handful got too mushy and pulpy, I slathered the pulp all over the steak and grabbed another handful of leaves, stem and petals. Soon, the steak was marinated in all the flower juice I could make.

I picked up the steak and walked back down to the bottom of the seating area. With effort, I dragged the steak up and over the wall and dropped it onto the arena floor right in front of the lion. The lion wasted no time. It pounced on the steak and ripped a huge bite out of it, swallowing hard. Then it ripped out another chunk and swallowed.

I looked at the clock. *2:17:05:21.4*. OK, eat. Eat faster. "Eat faster, you dumb cat!" I yelled. Half the steak was already gone when the lion figured out something was up. At first, it just shook its head back and forth. Then it started pawing at its snout. When it did that, its claws scratched its nose and lips, making little lines of blood start trickling over its face and down its paws. Finally, the cat started swaying back and forth. It roared, long and loud. It felt like the entire arena would collapse because the roar was shaking it so much. The lion roared again, this time softer.

Finally, the big cat fell over. It landed so hard the entire arena shook and I was almost positive it really would collapse this time. It didn't but a few of the loose stones I had used to climb the arena wall tumbled down and landed in the dirt next to the lion. The lion was panting hard. But then it wasn't. Its breaths came slower and slower and slower. Then the body of the lion shook, stiffened and stopped.

I waited. It didn't move. I climbed back down the wall. Much easier than going up, even with some of the stones missing. The lion didn't move. I walked over to it. It still didn't move. I pushed on its side gently with my foot and the lion didn't even whimper. I knew I was good; the lion had died.

"Yes!" I screamed, pumping one hand in the air. Then I remembered. I need the hide, not the lion. Shoot. Now I have to skin it. With what?

Its claws cut its face. I grabbed one of the lion's back paws and dragged it up until it reached the lion's belly and pushed. The claw went right through the fur and skin. I moved the paw around as much as possible, cutting a huge oval in the fur. It was messy and gross, what looked like blood oozed slightly from where I cut the skin. Then I set the paw down and grabbed hold of the cut fur. I had never skinned an animal, so I had no idea what I was doing. I pulled and pulled. There were some squishing sounds, and more oozy stuff, as the fur came loose a little bit. I pulled harder and more fur came loose. One more giant tug and the whole oval I had cut ripped off the animal. I fell back on my bottom and sat there, clutching the fur pelt.

This close up I realized how beautiful the lion had been, now that it wasn't trying to eat me. I had killed it though. A beautiful, majestic lion and I killed it for some test. My humanity in me shamed me for what I had done, and had done with absolutely no second thoughts. Tears welled up and I patted the lion's head. "I'm sorry," I told it. "I'm so sorry."

I couldn't do it any more. I took the part of the pelt I had already removed and walked over to the starting line. I dropped the pelt on the carpet square and looked at the plaque. "Nope," I said. "I won't degrade that animal any more. It's this or nothing. I'll fail before I cut into that gorgeous beast again. What I have already done is shameful and a disgrace, I won't do any more."

Behind me, the door to the main area of the Trials Arena clicked open. The timer stopped at *1:23:58:19.5*. Either the test heard me and accepted my answer or allowed me to just exit since I admitted defeat. I turned to walk out of the test door and heard a wuffling sound. I looked back and there was the lion, up and walking back to the gate it had first came out of. It was alive again and the spot I had cut was healed like nothing even happened. I looked back at the plaque. "Thank you," I told it. The room responded by shutting off the lights, all but the original spotlight on just the starting square. I walked out of the door, back into the dimly lit hallway where Dad was waiting.

The timer in the hallway showed *11:01:18:59:19.5* and was still counting down. I wasn't out, I didn't fail. But somehow had used more time on the outside than the timer inside the test showed. I gestured to the timer to ask Dad, but my voice failed. I was exhausted.

Dad figured out what I was saying. He handed me a bottle of water, which I guzzled down, and said, "Just like it is still going now, as we talk, the timer out here moves while you read the directions in there, and while you enter and exit the rooms. So, you have no time to spare."

I finished the water, and handed the bottle back to Dad. The second door on the right creaked open. No breaks, OK. I sighed, then thought. Not human, human needs don't apply here, Dad said. I am not tired. Just winded. I can do this. I rolled my eyes and went to the second door.

Inside was the same purple square carpet lit up like the first room, with the same bronze plaque and timer. The timer had *1:00:00:00:00.0* on it. Another week to complete this task. I looked at the plaque.

Test Two: Defeat the snake.
Careful! The venom hurts!

OK, a venomous snake. The lion was huge, so I wondered how big the snake would be. Well, time was ticking. I stepped off the carpet square and the room lit up. Except this time, it wasn't an arena. It was a clearing in the woods. And someone was screaming that wasn't me.

"Grab the sword! Grab the sword and cut off a head!" the voice yelled.

I followed the yelling around a tree and saw a guy standing there. He looked human enough, maybe only a few years older than me, caramel brown skin with brown curly hair and frantic, brown eyes. He looked like he had at one time been wearing a plain yellow T-shirt and jeans, but both pieces of clothing had so many burn holes and tatters that they hung from him in rags. He was waving around a flaming torch. An actual, old school, grab your torch and pitchforks, let's get the ogre, torch. He was waving the torch at a snake head that dipped down towards him. It looked like a normal green snake head, only huge of course. The snake head dripped venom that splashed on the ground and sizzled there, burning into the dirt, old leaves and other debris that made up the forest floor. The man moved the torch towards the snake head and the snake reared back. I followed the snake's movement back up...

Where it rejoined the other eight snake heads. Great. Nine heads, one body, some unidentifiable sizzling venom, what could go wrong? Defeat the snake sounded easy enough. No one told me it had nine heads. Fun.

The man was still screaming at me. "What's the matter with you? Grab the sword! We're all gonna die. Grab the bleeding sword!"

I looked where the man was gesturing with his empty hand. Leaning against a tree were two shining swords. I ran over and grabbed them, but then I stopped. I didn't want to kill a gorgeous mythical beast. I wouldn't and if the tests wanted me to just kill things, well it could kiss my behind.

But the lion didn't really die. It regenerated. So, did it count as killing if the animal regenerated? And could I assume the snake, or would it be snakes, will too since the lion did?

While I contemplated my moral dilemma, another snake head dipped down towards the man. Before he could force it back with the fire, a tiny drop of venom landed on the arm he had used to point to the swords.

He screamed in pain and I watched the skin where the venom landed bubble and boil. OK, moral decision made. This snake was actively attacking another person. Me here for the test? I was asking for it. He was just a random dude. I decided it was OK to kill the beast, and assume it would regenerate, to save another person's life.

I grabbed both swords and ran over to the man. One sword I dropped into the dirt. The other I grabbed by the hilt with both hands. He was telling me to cut off a head. I had never held a sword before, but I was willing to give it my best shot. I watched the snake bob and weave its heads. When one was close enough, I lunged forward, jumped, and swung the sword. And missed completely. Shut up, OK? I was new at this.

Another head bobbed down. This time I swung and made contact. The sword bit into the neck of that head, and when the snake jerked the head back in pain, it jerked me with it, still holding on to the sword. I pushed and pulled and jerked and bobbed. Finally, the sword sliced through the neck. One head of the snake and I came crashing to the ground together with a large thud. Oof. The hip I landed on with the lion! There was gonna be a bruise there later, probably a large one in full technicolor.

I looked up at the snake where it was missing a head. If they drooled venom, maybe their blood was venom too. I didn't want any drops of skin-boiling blood dripping on me. The blood was not dripping but bubbling. It was plopping and drooping and turning to solid? As I watched, the blood twisted around itself until it formed two new necks and two new heads. Now there were ten heads.

"What in the holy goats!" I screamed, "How…"

The man moved closer to me, close enough to use the fire to defend us both.

"Here," he said, gesturing to me with the torch. I took the torch and he took my sword. Then he held the sword over the fire until it was red hot. Then, he pressed the hot sword against the spot on his arm where the venom had landed, cauterizing the wound. I could see other spots on his body where he had done this before.

As he treated his wound, we talked. "Didn't know it did that, did you? There were seven heads when I got here."

I looked at him, incredulous. "You tried that twice? Why?"

The man shrugged. "I wanted to see what would happen if I cut off the head closer to the body." OK, makes sense, I guess. But why have me do it a third time?

I didn't ask him that. I should have, but instead I asked, "So, why do you stay here if you can't kill it?"

"Because I volunteered," he replied. "I'm from that village down there." The man pointed behind us, and I looked back, past where the door let me in. There was the plaque and the timer. Past them there were trees that got larger and denser as the ground sloped downward into a valley. Further down the mountain, I could see a river and a small village bordering it. The village seemed like something out of a storybook, with multi-level buildings made out of timber and mud plaster, with thatched roofs, all close together with cobblestone or dirt roads running in a wheel and spoke pattern out from the center of town. "I stay here to keep the snake from getting to the village. I will stay here until either we figure out a way to kill it, or it kills me and someone else gets to come up and try."

I thought for a moment. "Have you tried stabbing it in the heart, like from underneath?"

The man rolled his eyes. "Oh geez, why didn't we ever think of that?" he said sarcastically.

"Sorry, dang," I said defensively. "I didn't know. Maybe you hadn't been able to do it with only one person. Just trying to help."

The man sighed, his shoulders dropping slightly. "I know. Sorry, I shouldn't have snapped. It's been a long week, if you can't tell. I'm Ben, by the way."

"Bella," I answered. We didn't bother trying to shake hands or anything so formal as that. We were still dodging heads and venom, and poking back with the fire while we talked. Ben took the fire from me and motioned for me to grab the other sword.

I had to think. Can't cut off the heads, because two more grow back from the blood. Can't kill it from underneath, Ben had tried apparently. I tried to think of a solution. The lion was hungry. I gave him tainted food and he ate it and died. Then I got the hide I needed for the test. This test was just to defeat the snake. I didn't even need to kill it technically, just defeat it. Maybe if I could figure out what the snake wanted, I could figure out how to defeat it?

I asked Ben if he had any ideas. "What d'ya mean what does it want? It wants to kill us!" he replied.

"Yeah, but why?" I pushed. "Is it just hungry and sees us as food? 'Cuz maybe if that's true we can just get it food and it will stop. What does it want?"

Ben looked at me, squinting his eyes. "You're not from around here, are you?" I shook my head no. He sighed, and kept talking. "Then let me educate you. These things have no motivation. They kill because they can. They don't eat the dead. They don't use anything or take anything. They just roar and kill and move on to the next town."

"They?" I asked. "There's more than one of these?"

"Yeah," Ben replied. "There are a lot of them."

"Where are the rest? Is this a boy snake thing or a girl snake thing? How do they mate? Do they partner for life?" I pelted questions at Ben, an idea forming.

Ben shouted at me, "Do I look like a freaking herpetologist? How the hell should I know all that stuff? All I know is that there are a bunch of these things around the world, and if you find one sleeping, don't wake it up. Run away as fast as you can. They sleep for a long time. But when they wake up, they rampage and kill indiscriminately. Then somehow or another, they find a new place, get tired and go to sleep again."

Thoughts were running through my head. Why do they wake up? What makes them go to sleep? Would sleeping count as defeated? Well, if nothing else, sleeping would make it easier to find a way to kill while still protecting the village.

I needed to know more about these snakes. I couldn't defeat it if I didn't know what it wanted. While I thought, Ben had been defending us. I hadn't been paying attention very well when I felt a big glob of something hit my left shoulder.

The glob felt cool and slimy. Then it felt hot. Very hot. "Oh my god, it's burning me!" I screamed. I looked at my shoulder and a drop of venom was sinking into my skin, making it boil.

Ben looked over as I screamed. He quickly took the sword in his hand, heated it up over the torch and pushed it onto my shoulder. That was worse somehow. I screamed again.

"Hold on, hold on," Ben said, actually kind of nicely. "The heat will burn the nerve soon." It must have because suddenly it didn't burn any more. It throbbed and was definitely painful, but it wasn't burning. "There." Ben rubbed the spot he had cauterized with his hand. It was a friendly gesture so I didn't tell him that his rubbing it smarted a bunch.

I looked at my shoulder. That was gonna leave a nasty scar. "Thanks," I told Ben. Then I decided to take a risk. "I am gonna wander over that way for a minute. I'm not leaving," I added when Ben looked rather panicked. "I'll be right back. I just have to do something for a second."

I walked back around a big tree. I could be wrong, using It like this, but I didn't know what else to do. I needed a book about these types of snakes. I needed to know about them quickly and as much as possible. I looked for my ice and warm. The door plopped down in front of me just like with the lion. I opened it, and there was a book, open to a page with the header 'Bi-headed Venomous Snakes'. Sounds about right. I grabbed the book and read the page.

Bi-Headed Venomous Snakes

The bi-headed snake is native to the European warmer climates, but have migrated all over the world. Such snakes travel in pairs. Do not fear the bi-headed snake if there are two. They are only dangerous when alone. The snakes need one another to maintain proper body temperatures. Bi-heads often sleep for long periods, as long as one hundred years. The partnered pair will sleep coiled around each other for warmth inside caves. Due to their unusual number of heads, many people will not be able to tell how many bi-heads are present in a cave and will assume either only one is present, if they know of their regenerative power, or many, if they don't. Bi-head blood can heal any injuries the animal may sustain. Any wound inflicted that causes bleeding will repair itself, and the bi-head will cause bleeding to heal a non-hemorrhagic wound. While awake, a bi-head will replace a lost head twice over. Their venom is acidic, able to eat through metal, wood or stone and lethal to living things. Bi-heads do not consume food, but make energy from the sun. This energy does not convert to warmth, so alone, a bi-head will get cold very quickly. Cold bi-heads become unstable and seem angry. The warmth of fire is too much for a bi-head and they will move away from it. They desire light, not heat, unless it is from another bi-head. Once paired, bi-heads will peacefully find a cave or cavern to sleep in. Sleep is restorative for bi-heads. During sleep, any excess heads beyond two will disintegrate. Also, the venomous saliva of a bi-head dries while it sleeps. On occasion, one bi-head will awaken before its partner and head out of the cave. This is dangerous for all surrounding humans and animals. The bi-head alone will not stray far from its partner. When sufficiently cold, or when the partner wakes and calls for its lost mate, the lone bi-head will return to the cave. There is no known way to kill a bi-head. Bi-head reproduction is not understood at this time.

Well, that was helpful. Really helpful. I threw the book back through the door and the door popped away. I ran back to Ben, yelling, "Are there caves nearby?"

"What?" he asked when I got closer.

I panted a little. "Are there caves nearby? His mate would be in a cave somewhere close."

"Yeah," Ben answered, waving the fire at another dipping head and jumping out of the way of a venom drop.

Don't point towards the village, don't point towards the village. Ben pointed away from the village, to the north and a little east. "Over that way," he told me. "You ask a lot of weird questions."

I started running the way Ben pointed. "The snake should start moving this way soon," I called out over my shoulder. "Let it!"

Ben was yelling something back, but I was too far away to hear. I was running as fast as I could. The forest got thicker as I ran. Soon I was dodging low hanging branches and trying to make sure I didn't trip over roots and break my ankle. I don't need oxygen, I had to keep reminding myself, and I pushed to run faster. I was not sure if that one was strictly true, Dad never said that, but if it worked, it worked. I didn't want to leave Ben alone with that bi-head for too long. He had looked almost completely done in when I first arrived and I wasn't sure he would make it much longer on his own.

About the time I thought my lungs would explode, I saw a cave to my left. I ran to it, then slowed down to survey the area. The cave entrance was not very large. I would have had to duck to get into it. How did that huge snake fit? I hoped this was the right cave. Above the cave, a small hill was formed with large boulders. The ground was sloping and not very straight underneath them, but the large rocks made the hill look smooth and rounded. They looked like maybe one good push...

I stepped inside the cave. Right near the entrance, far enough back not to be seen from outside the cave, but close enough that the sunlight still dappled over its skin, was a second bi-headed snake. This one only had two heads and wasn't dripping venom from its mouth.

I had to wake up this snake so it would call its partner home. I was some kind of stupid. I didn't even think about it. I just picked up a stick and poked the thing. One head shot up, and a red eye came level with my head. My brain caught up with me then and I bolted out of the cave. I climbed up the hill, perching myself on top of one of the boulders directly on top of the cave mouth and watched the opening. Slowly, one snake head emerged from the opening, then the other. One head looked east, one west. Then one looked north and one south. Then the mouths of both heads opened and hissed.

The hiss was so quiet. One of the heads hissed in a high soprano. The other head hissed in a low alto. The two tones match so perfectly that it sounded like a song. A sad song. There was no way the other bi-head could hear this all the way over where I had left Ben. But I was entranced by the song. I wanted to go down to the snake, hug it, keep it warm and love it all of its days.

I shook my head to clear my mind. What was wrong with me? That song must have some sort of magical power. As I listened, this time aware of its power and defending myself against it, I heard something else. The woods around me were crunching. I scanned around to see where the crunching sound was coming from.

It was the other bi-head, sliding towards the cave! It had heard its partner's song and came running, or well, slithering. The two bi-heads met at the cave opening and they rubbed their heads on one another, as if checking if each other was OK or warming each other up. Kind of like when you rub your hands together when they are cold. Ben was coming up behind the snakes and I motioned at him to come around and join me on the boulder. He climbed up and we both watched as the two snakes twined around each other, rubbed their heads together and eventually both slid back into the cave.

"OK," I whispered to Ben, and started moving off the boulder we were sitting on. "Help me."

I went to the back of the boulder, near the corner of the back and side of it, and braced my hands on it, twisting my feet in the dirt to stabilize myself. Ben looked at me, confused. I gestured that we were going to push the boulder off the top of the cave in front of the cave opening. I would have just said it, but I didn't want the two now very awake snakes to hear me. The book indicated they were docile in pairs, but I was only willing to trust the book so much.

Ben nodded his head at me to show he understood and copied my movements on the other backside corner of the boulder. I started pushing against my side, and

Ben pushed his. Slowly, ever so slowly, the boulder started to wiggle free. I pushed harder, then Ben pushed harder. We took turns pushing our corner, wiggling the boulder the way a little kid wiggles a loose tooth, back and forth. The boulder wiggled more. I took a deep breath and pushed one more time. The boulder popped free and rolled off the top and directly into the space just before the opening of the cave.

With that boulder gone, the perfect stack of stones that made the rounded hill wasn't balanced right any more. The rest of the boulders, large stones, and small stones started rolling after it in an avalanche. I ran backwards, narrowly escaping being taken over the edge myself. When the dust and dirt settled, the entire cave opening was blocked by stones. No sunlight could get into it to feed the bi-heads.

I looked over what used to be the top of the hill at Ben. His mouth was hanging open in surprise. I think he really thought he would just die fighting that thing. Ben started to laugh as it settled in his mind that he wasn't going to die after all.

I laughed with him. I had done it. I had defeated the snake before the timer… The timer!! I had no idea how much time had passed, but based on the lion, way more than I thought probably.

I took off at a dead run. Tree branches snapped across my face and I didn't even dodge them. Oh no, oh no, oh no. How much time was left? Through the trees, I started to be able to make out the red shimmer of the timer. I kept running. Finally, I reached the clearing and could read the timer clearly. *45:23:01.1*! Crap, I had used almost the whole week!

I got to the square carpet and stopped, standing on it. The timer kept counting down. Where's the door? Where's the fecking door? I yelled at the timer, "Stop! I did it! I defeated the snake. Where's the door?" I started jumping up and down on the square, angry. *40:01:59.3*, for cripe's sake. Only forty minutes left. Ben ran past me, still laughing. As he went by, he stopped and reached out to hug me.

"Thank you, thank you!" he cried. I reached out to him as well, and he stepped forward onto the carpet square and hugged me tight. A creak sounded behind us. I turned and saw the door. The timer had stopped at *37:10:43.9*. I was not sure if the timer was waiting for Ben to join me or if something had been happening with the bi-heads that had to finish before the timer would say I was done. I would not think about the fact that the timer was actually probably waiting for the bi-heads to die, so I just assumed I had been waiting for Ben. Either way, the timer with Dad was still running, so I needed to get a move on. I stepped away from Ben and slipped through the door, back into the hallway with Dad. I looked back through the Test Two door and saw Ben brandishing the torch again, fighting a nine-headed snake.

As I stepped into the hallway again, Dad handed me another water and a strawberry Pop-Tart he had pulled out of his pocket. "Cutting it close, Bella Bella," he said.

I took a swig of water and ate half the Pop-Tart before I replied, "If that stupid timer would just act right, I wouldn't have this problem."

Dad laughed. I bit the Pop-Tart again and looked at my shoulder where the venom had hit me. Nothing. OK, guess I reset too. Gods, I was tired. Why was I doing this again? At that moment, I really couldn't think of a valid enough reason. Then I remembered the big doors that slammed shut over the building. So, either I kept going or I sat here with Dad and chilled for the next... I looked at the timer again, a little over ten weeks, or until the Trials decided I failed. That almost sounded better than this insanium.

"Remember Bella," Dad was talking while I contemplated quitting. "Time doesn't..."

"Work the same, here," we both said at the same time.

I drank the last of my water, decided if I was stuck here, I might as well keep trying, and told Dad, "I know, I know." I walked over to the third door on the right and waited for it to come open. "Let's just do this."

"Attagirl!" I heard Dad say as the door opened and I stepped through.

Same as before, small light, square of carpet, timer with *1:00:00:00:00.0* on it, and a plaque. I read the plaque:

Test Three: Put the deer back in the pen. Don't hurt the cutie!

All right, no killing this time. But deer is both the singular and the plural. How many deer were we talking about here?

I stepped off the mat. Why waste time thinking? I only had one week and I couldn't know the answer to that until I started the test.

In front of me, was another clearing in another forest. This forest was different, though. The trees were smaller than in the last one and there wasn't as much detritus on the forest floor. More pine needles and less leaves. There was also a small hut in the clearing made of stone. It was like a painting. There was a small trail of smoke coming out of the fireplace, a split rail fence making a small enclosed area to one side of the door, and a woman standing in the doorway, looking left and right, high and low.

I walked over to the woman. "Are you looking for something?" I asked.

"My baby," she replied. "Little CeCe." She cupped her hands around her mouth and loudly yelled, "CeCe! CeCe! Where are you?"

OK, a picture was forming here. "Is CeCe by any chance," I said slowly, "a deer?"

The woman looked at me when I said this. "Yes, she is! Have you seen her? No bigger than a fawn, the prettiest little thing, you can't miss her."

I sighed. For some reason, this test bugged me. I am looking for a woman's lost pet deer? Really? The other two tests wanted to kill me and this time I was looking for a lost pet? "Does CeCe happen to have fangs or claws or venom or something?"

The woman looked startled. "No, why would you think that? She's a deer. She's harmless and so friendly."

Run of the mill lost pet, check. I looked closer at the woman. She was wearing a long piece of cloth draped over her. It was silk or something shimmery. The cloth was wound around her body like a dress and cinched at the waist with a golden belt. Hanging from the belt were three separate knives, each a different length and width. She had long golden hair and pale skin, with perfect rosy cheeks and ruby lips. She was tall and slender, her face seemed radiant but worried. Next to her, propped on the door frame, was a bow and some arrows. I got the idea the pet may be run of the mill, but the person wasn't. Something told me this was not supposed to be a human person, but it wasn't actually a god either. Maybe a replica of a god, used for the tests.

"Does CeCe have any favorite treats?" I asked.

"Oh yes," replied the woman. "She loves red clover and chestnuts."

"Do you have either of those, in like a bag or something?" I felt like I was talking to someone just a little simple. This task seemed just a little too simple. Something was either off or the Trials was giving a little break for still being alive.

The woman darted inside the cabin and came back with a small burlap bag, just big enough to fit in your palm, full of chestnuts. I took it from her and started to shake it, the way you shake cat treats to get your pet cat to scurry over and play with you. The woman kept calling out for CeCe while I shook the bag.

I looked back at the timer. It had only been thirty minutes. OK, not bad, but this obviously wasn't working. "You said she liked red clover too. Is there any of that nearby?" I sought out my ice and warm feeling. Maybe it could help me not feel so gripey. I found it and toyed with it a little bit. It helped. I relaxed.

The woman looked at me hard, and ran into the cabin. She came back with a piece of paper and spread it on the ground between us. "There is a red clover patch here." She circled a spot on the paper, which was actually a map. "And here, and here, and here." The woman was talking and moving rapidly, circling every red clover patch within a hundred miles.

What was her problem? Then it dawned on me, or really It dawned on me. Without meaning to, I had compelled the woman to tell me everything. I was just using It to calm myself but she felt it as a compulsion for truth. I let go of my ice and warm feeling, and the woman visibly relaxed.

"OK," I told her. "Thank you. Why don't you stay here and watch for CeCe to return? I will check out some of these closer patches to see if she wandered away for a snack."

I took the map, tucked the bag of chestnuts in my pocket, and walked away, trying to figure out which way was north. I assumed the sun still rose in the east and set in the west, so I looked up. Wait. What time is it?

I called back to the woman still standing in the doorway, "What time is it?"

"Just after breakfast, why?" she replied.

I waved off answering her, and looked up at the sky. There, the sun above the horizon, just peeking through the trees. That must be east. I turned the map in my hands so east on the map was facing the same way as the sun and I was facing north. The closest patch of red clover was in front of me, due north, and a little west. I started walking.

I probably should have run, but I didn't. I figured a small deer probably spooked easy, and I needed to walk quietly or I would scare it away even if it was at the first patch I came to. After a few minutes, I came to a large clearing. There was red clover everywhere.

I took the bag of chestnuts out of my pocket and shook them a bit. In the center of the clearing, a small head popped up. No way, too easy.

I shook the bag again and took a few tentative steps toward the deer. It looked at me, frozen in its tracks. I slowly kept it up. Shake the bag, walk a few steps. Shake the bag, walk a few steps. Soon I was close enough to make out the whole deer. She really was a pretty little thing.

There was a rope tied around the deer's neck, like a leash. The end was frayed and I assumed that was how CeCe the deer got free. Her leash broke. If I could only get close enough to grab the broken leash, I'd be home free.

A thought came to me. When Dad glowed, I wanted to move closer to him. He told me that when I glowed, he felt the same way. I felt for my ice and warm, focusing on drawing CeCe the deer closer to me. I didn't need truth, I needed to touch her.

I tried to keep things really calm. Not too much It, but just a touch. Shake the bag, walk a few steps. Before I knew it, CeCe was stepping closer to me. And then she nuzzled her face into my hand.

"Holy crap," I breathed quietly. With one hand, I lowered the bag of chestnuts so CeCe could dive into them. With the other, I gently grabbed the end of the rope leash. There! I had it.

I clicked my tongue a few times like I've seen people do with horses. "C'mon, CeCe. Let's take you back to Mommy," I said gently. When I pulled on the leash, the deer complied and we walked back to the cabin. The poor thing was going to have a stomach ache later because I let her eat all the chestnuts as we walked, but who cares? I brought her back and it only took…

Two days. I saw the timer and couldn't believe it. It had only been two days and here I was, handing CeCe back over to the woman. She was gushing out thank yous, and 'Oh my pretty girl, don't scare me like that', but I ignored her ramblings.

"You're welcome. It's fine," I mumbled in response, handing over the leash. "Maybe try a metal chain instead of rope for her." The woman took the leash, and led CeCe into the pen.

I walked away, back towards the carpet square. No way would the door appear. No way. I stepped on the carpet and heard the creak of the door opening. The timer stopped at *4:22:54:33.6*. Just a tad over two days. No way. I walked out the door and didn't look back. I wasn't giving the Trials a hint of a chance to change their minds. This test was done and dusted.

When I entered the dim hallway, Dad was dusting one of the sconces further down the hallway. He heard the door close behind me and turned to stare at me. His face dropped in surprise.

"How?" he stumbled. "In…" Dad looked at the timer, "two days? Two days!" Dad sat down on the floor hard and put his hands on his head.

"Dad," I said, unsure why he was acting like this. "It was easy. I just talked to the lady, got the snacks, and found the deer. It came back with me 'cuz I had the chestnuts."

Dad stood up quickly. "Easy? It was easy?" he exclaimed. "I almost failed that one! Wait, wait, hold on a second. She talked to you?"

Dad almost failed that? How? "Yeah, I walked up and she looked all concerned. So, I asked her what was up and she told me all about CeCe. So, I found CeCe for her."

Dad ran a hand down his face. "Wow, she talked to you. And didn't try to kill you?" Duh. Dad kept talking. "Well I guess don't look a gift horse in the mouth. We needed extra time."

The door to the fourth room opened. Dad and I both looked at it. "Well," he sighed. "Get going."

I walked through the fourth door to the same set up as before, and read the plaque:

Test Four: One Boar, Wanted Alive, Not Dead!

Again, no killing. But this time, the plaque made it seem as if killing the boar would be the easier solution. The plaque said that the boar was wanted, but who was it wanted by? Would this be another lost pet? The way it was written reminded me of the wanted posters from old western movies, where they had to catch an outlaw and bring them to justice. So probably not a pet, but an animal that was doing something bad. All right, boars are just big pigs with tusks and mean, right? How hard could it be to trap? First, I had to see how big is big and how angry those tusks were.

I stepped off the starting square and this time, I was on a tall mountain. Looking up, the mountain rose high into the clouds, snow covering its peak. Below me, the mountain ran down into an idyllic valley with a town and a river and green grass everywhere. This was not the same town as the test with the bi-head snakes. The mountain was much larger, with bigger trees. The town was much smaller and the homes were very different too, made from stone with tile roofs instead of wood and thatched roofs. Around me, there were large and small trees, lots of thick undergrowth, scrub brush, and debris on the forest floor. And lots of trampled foliage.

As I looked around, I heard a loud thunderous hammering. I looked for the source of the sound. It wasn't hard to find. A very large boar was running down the mountainside, leaving broken trees, churned up debris and squished flowers and bushes in its wake. It was not as big as I thought but bigger than I hoped, standing about shoulder height on me. I watched as the boar continued down the mountain, went into the valley, through the town and just made a mess out of everything. Fences were knocked over, carts in the market place overturned, and people and animals had been knocked about. Even from this far away, I could hear people crying in the town and see them running around, trying to defend their stuff.

After a while of rampaging, the boar wandered back up the mountain. I followed it, and saw it go almost up into the snowy top of the mountain. Just before it got to where the air would be too cold and thin, the boar stopped and laid down in a sunny patch where the snow was not too thick, pulling bits of animal (but not human, please say not human) off its tusks and munched on the meat. The bits of meat had been living things that got in the way of the rampaging boar's huge tusks and were gored while the boar had run around all crazy. He made it his supper. Then he fell asleep snoring.

Maybe this would be easy too. If I could just catch him sleeping, maybe all I would need was a good strong rope to pull him over to the starting area, or wherever it should go. I glanced down into the village to see if maybe I should be capturing the boar and taking it there. But as I walked down to investigate, I could see that there were signs all over town offering a reward for the boar's head. I definitely didn't want to take it there, then. The plaque had said the boar had to be delivered alive, but the townspeople would just kill it if I took him there. The starting square it must be, then, I assumed.

I started walking toward the sleeping boar. Nope, no such luck of an easy capture while it was asleep. I took one step and the boar woke up, and woke up mad! He ran around crazy again, down the mountain, through the valley, over the village and then walked back up again. He ate his new snacks and slept.

Huh, interesting. What to do? I looked at the path of destruction the boar made. It was almost identical both times. In fact, there was only one path of rampage down the mountain. It was maybe twenty feet wide. But other than that path, the forest was healthy and thriving. The starting square was dead center to the boar's path about halfway down the mountain.

I had an idea forming. I would need a net. A very big net. But first, I should warn the people, get them out of the way of my plan. I ran down the mountain to the village. I talked first to one person, then another. They all shrugged me off. They wouldn't abandon their homes. They would stay, have them smashed to bits, then rebuild, just to have it all smashed to bits again.

Ugh, I didn't have time for this! "You are not abandoning your homes!" I cried out. "You just have to leave for a little while. Then when all this is done, you will rebuild for the last time! Give me a day, one day, please."

The people finally understood. I think. Or maybe I used some of It unintentionally and compelled them to leave rather than to come. Either way, they were leaving, albeit they couldn't understand why I didn't just kill the boar for them. I wasn't wasting more time to explain it to them, not that I thought they would understand that they were all just a part of a test in an old wooden barn in the heavens and not real anyway. On to stage two.

I ran back up the mountain to the boar, and stomped, hard, on the ground near him. He woke up, went nuts down the mountain again, and again climbed back up to try to sleep. But I wouldn't let him. I stomped again. And again, down he went and back up. Ten times

I did this, twenty. Every time the boar came back up the mountain and had just laid down, I would stomp near him to wake him up again. He was getting ragged, and tired, I could tell. But he never deviated from that twenty-foot-wide section of the forest.

Time for stage three. While the boar was racing down the mountain, I called on It. I needed a net, twenty feet wide, twenty feet tall, spread out and tied to the healthy trees, with the starting square directly in the middle. The ice and warm in my center quivered. A door was supposed to bring what I asked for, but how does a door set up a net? I checked my time. *3:22:15:27.8*, still plenty. I looked to my ice and warm again and got more insistent. I didn't care, I wanted that net, set up for me if you will.

The biggest door I have ever seen in my life plopped down. Still black with the white handle, but huge. Bigger than the net I was asking for. I pulled on the handle, and the door flew open. A net made out of metal chain mesh flew out and bound itself to the trees, just how I had asked. As soon as the net was set, the door popped away, leaving me feeling like It was angry at me. What? I shrugged. I needed it. And it's not like anyone gave me rules saying I couldn't ask for that. It's not like anyone really gave me any rules at all.

By the time the net was set, the boar was back at the top of the mountain again, huffing and panting, and ready to just sleep. One more stomp. Up you get, Mr Boar. One more run. The boar was clumsy and tired. He stumbled more than he rampaged. Right into my net. As soon as he touched it, the boar became very angry. His path was blocked. He thrashed against the net, but his tusks had gotten caught in the mesh and all the pulling and shaking of his head in the world would not get them free. He tried to run away, just taking the net with him, but I ran to the trees on one side of the net and gathered the ends in my hands. I quickly walked towards the other end of the net. The net circled round behind me, making a pincer around the boar. I passed the starting square and got closer to the net still attached to the trees, closing the pincer. When I got to the trees still attached to the net, I ducked under their ties and the net in my hands followed me. The net now made a full circle. The boar had nowhere to go and no energy to fight me, although he did try.

Slowly, I walked back towards the starting square. As I did, the circle the net made got smaller and smaller. Once I crossed the starting square again, I lifted up the net and went over and under it until I formed a loose knot. Then I started the process again, going back to the trees holding the net, under the net, back to the starting square, and back to the trees. I circled and circled the boar, tying the net up tight around him, pushing him towards the starting square. I would duck under the net, circle again, duck and circle, getting closer and closer.

Eventually, I was right up to the boar. I could reach out and touch him. And he was pacing back and forth over the starting square. He was close enough. I threw the wound-up net still remaining in my hands over the boar and wrestled him onto the starting square. He bucked and he fought, throwing his head with those huge tusks around, but he just didn't have any energy left. Finally, he submitted, lying down on the starting square, breathing hard. As the door creaked open, the boar shook his head one last time.

One of the tusks got me right in my stomach. I rolled away, out the door and into the main hallway where Dad was, screaming in pain. Blood was pouring out of me. I was dying. I crawled away from the door and further into the dim hallway. Crying and scrambling about for anything to stop the bleeding, I called out for my dad, who came running.

"Bella! What is it? What happened?" Dad grabbed my shoulders to stop me thrashing.

"The boar!" I screamed. "The boar's tusk gored me. Daddy, I'm gonna die. I'm bleeding. Help me!"

Dad started pulling on my arms, but my hands were covering my wound. I was sure they were literally holding my intestines inside me. "Bella, stop. Bella, let go," Dad kept saying. "Bella. Bella! Look, you're fine. Look."

I finally stopped and looked. When I pulled my hands away, they were sticky with blood. There was a huge tear in my shirt, but no hole in me. I remembered the venom burn. I healed. How did I heal?

"You can't die in the Trials, Bella," Dad said. "They made them that way on purpose. You can fail.

You can get an injury that would mean death in the real world, but the Trial Arena heals you first and you just fail the test. But it wouldn't be fair to let people die here."

I listened to him and knew I had failed rather than die. That injury in the real world? No coming back. So, I must have failed. "I'm sorry, Dad," I whispered. "I had him, I was there. The door had already opened and everything. But he turned his head and his tusk got me. I failed, I'm sorry."

"Bella, look at the timer." I looked where Dad was pointing. The timer was at *9:01:17:37:07.6* and still counting down.

"How, Dad? That would have killed me in real life," I asked.

Dad chuckled, pulled me sitting up and wrapped me in a hug. "The boar gored you after you finished the test. After, Bella," he said, holding me tight. "The door was open for you to leave so the test was over already. It can't count what happens after. That was a fluke, a glitch in the programming. The boar was resetting and it didn't intend for you to be so close when it did. It doesn't count."

I knew the timer was still running, and I had to get moving, but I wanted my dad to hold me for a little while longer. We sat there for a while, not sure how long, Dad holding me and rocking me. He held my face and stroked my hair, whispering, "My Bella. My strong, smart Bella."

After a bit, Dad leaned back and looked at my face. "You ready to go again," he asked. "You're almost halfway there."

I wiped my face and nodded. "Yeah." We stood up and I looked down at myself. I was a mess. Shirt torn and bloody, hands bloody, face was probably blotchy from crying and I could feel the rats' nest my hair had become. But it didn't matter.

I took a deep breath and walked up to the fifth door. It clicked open. I took another deep breath, blew it out and then walked through.

It was the same set up, with one slight difference. The timer only read *1:00:00:00.0*. One day, I only got one day for this one. Thinking about the other tests and how long they took, I wondered what could take only one day. I read the plaque:

Test Five: Clean the stables.

Well, that seemed easy enough. People on farms cleaned stables out every day and it only took a couple hours. I stepped off the starting square and even before the lights came on all the way, the smell hit me. When I say it hit me, I mean physically square in the face. I doubled over and almost threw up. The rank was so bad. The worst thing I ever smelled. My eyes watered and my nose started running. I pulled my ruined shirt off and tied it around my face. The coppery smell of my blood helped to dull the intensity of the putrid smell coming from the stables some, but not enough.

I was able to look around though. The stables were huge. A thousand pens for hundreds of different types of animals. Fortunately, all the pens were empty. Otherwise, I might have had to call someone for animal abuse, because even simulated animals, or whatever these tests used, did not deserve to be living in that nasty. The pens had to have been sitting, gathering filth for at least the last decade or two. It was thick on the floor, and hard, and just so gross.

There was no way. No possible way to clean a thousand pens this disgusting in one day. I needed more time. I had to have more time. But how?

"Time works different here," I heard my dad saying. He had said it how many times now? Time worked different for sure. It lied. Things that should only have taken me a day or an afternoon, took almost a week. Time lied. Time... lied. And I could make things tell the truth. Or at least compel them to. What if I made time stop lying in here? What if I made the timer tell the truth? My truth. What if it lied to everyone else instead of me?

I walked over to the timer. *23:45:27:18.6.* I felt the ice and warm. I made a bubble of it and flipped it inside out. Then I put the bubble around the timer.

23:45:27:17.4
23:45:27:17.4
23:45:27:17.4

23:45:27:17.3

It worked! Time hadn't stopped for me, just slowed way down.

No one taught me how It worked. Remember that. Dad kept talking about time as if it was this not real thing that could be manipulated. So, I manipulated it. Had I known what I did to everyone outside the testing room, I would have never done it. Had I known I was hurting people, I would have popped that bubble and found a different way. I swear! Please judge me on what I knew and not on what I didn't. I will forever feel ashamed for hurting all those innocent people. Punish me how you want. But please understand, it was never intentional and pains me every single day and will for the rest of my life. No matter your choice at the end of this, you will never be able to punish me more than I am constantly punishing myself.

With the time issue taken care of, I walked through the stables to evaluate my supplies. The stables themselves were made of old metal, but the stuff inside looked rather updated. It had electricity and heat ducts. There was some normal mucking stuff, brooms, shovels, pails, rakes, a lawnmower and leaf blower, lying around the stable's main door. I looked up at the roof of the stables. A sprinkler system. Hmm, might come in handy. I found a closet and looked inside. Jugs of cleaning solution concentrate, rags, trash bags and matches. Then I walked around the outside of the stables. There were metal barrels. Some were empty, some had water in it, or feed. Others had lye and leather tanning oils.

A plan was forming in my brain. A dangerous plan, very dangerous. I remembered an experiment we did in science class with lye. The teacher put a little lye in a dish with a chicken leg. Then he lit the Bunsen burner and placed the bowl over the flame. The lye heated up and ate through the chicken leg, bone and all, until it was just goop. Goop washes away easy.

DO NOT TRY THIS AT HOME, KIDS! I REPEAT: DO NOT TRY THIS! You will die, I should have died. In fact, take this as a general warning for everything you read. Don't try it. I did a lot of dumb shit that only worked because I am half not-human, and very, very lucky. Don't try any of it, but most especially DON'T TRY THIS!

It took a while to set everything up. I took the bottles of cleaning solution and ran down every aisle, dumping them on the floor and into every pen. Then, I pulled the metal barrels of lye, and the barrels of feed to the doorways of the stables. I put one of each barrel at each doorway. There were twenty doors, and twenty barrels of each, perfect. Then I took the empty barrels and laid two on their sides next to each other at each door to the stables, behind the lye, with the open part facing the doors. Then I went to the main stable doors and lit a match. I took a breath, pulled my T-shirt up tighter over my nose and threw the match into the stables.

The cleaning solution plus dung in the stables took off like tinder, burning hot and fast. Then I dumped the lye barrels in, running from doorway to doorway, kicking over lye barrels, so the lye ran into each pen of the stables. The fire was burning through the waste on the stable floors well, but so much hot lye started breaking down the organic material even faster. Once the lye was all spilled, I ran as far from the stables as I could. The smell, chemically and toxic, was heady and my eyes felt like they were melting.

As I predicted, the sprinkler system kicked on from the smoke. Lye and water make an extreme heat reaction. Even as far away as I was, the heat was intense. But fortunately, the sprinkler system was foam fire suppression instead of just water. If not, I probably would have gone boom. The sprinkler system put out the fire and settled the lye. When the temperature came down, I went back over to the stables and dumped the feed into the pens. The packed grain feed pellets expanded, soaking up any remaining liquids and the lye, leaving an easy to sweep up mess. I took out the leaf blower and blew the mess into piles by each of the stable doors. Then I went around to each door and swept up the piles into the empty barrels.

I could have died. I didn't, but I could have. I giggled because well, science is cool even when it almost kills you. I am still not sure today if what I did in the stables would have worked in real life, if I actually got all the sciencey bits rights, or if I just willed it into working instead of just blowing the stables up. But at that moment, all I was thinking was, 'Take that Science Olympiad team', and laughing at my stupid, dumb luck.

I figured that was probably clean enough, and went to the timer. *6:44:18.3*. Not bad. I took the bubble off the timer and stepped onto the starting square. I heard the door creak open, and as I stepped out, I realized I had made a very, very bad mistake. And not just by doing crazy, probably wrong, explosion science.

Dad was screaming. Not the, 'Yay, you did it', screaming I expected, but absolute pain and terror screaming.

"What did you do?" he shrieked as soon as I was out of the door. Dad was bent over double, holding his stomach and his head, crouching then standing, then tensing all over. "AnnaBella! What did you do?" Dad saw me and started over to me.

I had frozen in place just outside the door, struck by how he was acting. What was wrong with him? Why was he acting like he was in so much pain? "I finished, Dad. I passed the test," I said, breathlessly. I had never, ever seen Dad look at me that way. He looked at me like he was horrified and scared of me.

Dad's voice was hoarse. "But what did you DO?" He grabbed me by the shoulders and shook me hard, just for a second. "What did you do? What did you do? What the hell did you do to time!"

What did I do to time? What did he mean? I was inside the test, how could I do anything to... Oh my gods of all shapes and sizes! Did the bubble affect all time? Like, outside the test too? I thought...

Suddenly I was terrified. What had I done? "I put a bubble on the timer. I made it invert," I whispered.

"Invert?" Dad asked, then he looked like he suddenly got it. "Invert! You inverted time itself! How? How?"

Still whispering, I responded. "Time lied to me inside the tests. A few minutes were counted by the timer as whole days. So, I inverted it. I made it lie the other way. You said your power, my power, is to compel things to tell us the truth and come to us. So, I just pushed my power backwards and made the timer lie to me and time go away instead. The timer went too slow instead of too fast."

Dad crumpled on the floor. I was reaching panic attack, hyperventilating level. Dad was always stoic. Dad was always easy breezy. Dad was always casual even when everything was a mess. We could be in the middle of the apocalypse and Dad would have smiled, cracked a few jokes to lighten the mood, and would have a plan. Dad did NOT crumple on the floor and scream. Dad most definitely did not cry, but Dad was crying now.

"I'm sorry," he was whimpering. "Oh, I am so sorry. I should have done better. I should have taught her better. I didn't explain right. Don't blame her. It was me, it was my fault. Oh no, oh no. Please."

I knelt down and put a hand on his shoulder. "Dad? Dad? Daddy? Please, you're scaring me. What did I do?"

After a moment, Dad wiped his face with his hands, and took a huge, shuddering breath. "AnnaBella," he said, his voice still shaking. "You didn't slow down the timer. You slowed down time. All of time. Everywhere. I could think at normal speed but my body, my movements all slowed down. The gods would have felt it. The coordinators like me would have felt it. Humans, oh fuck, humans felt it." Dad looked shocked and horrified all over again. "Human hearts and breathing would have slowed down the same amount your timer did. They still would have needed their hearts to beat just as fast as normal, but you slowed time down, so they didn't. It would have been minutes instead of seconds between heartbeats for them. They would have felt it, known it was happening and been able to think in between each beat, feel the pain, the squeezing of needing the heart to beat again, but would not have been able to make it happen."

Slowly, my brain caught up with what Dad was saying. Oh, no. Oh, no, no, no, no. People, humans would die from that. Like, but it was everyone, everywhere? Did I just kill the whole human race? No. Wait. No. How? What? My brain exploded.

I needed out of here. I needed out. I ran to the door of the Trials Arena and started pounding on it. "Let me out! Oh god, what did I do? Let me out! I need out! I don't want to finish the Trials. Let me out, I have to fix this! Please!" The idea of what I did, or maybe did, became so heavy, I sank to the floor, still pounding and clawing on the door. My fists were bleeding from pounding so hard, scraping my hands on the old splintery wood. My words became unintelligible sobs. Blood and tears mixed on the floor in puddles as I kept beating the doors.

Exhaustion started to pull on me. I have no idea how long I sat there, beating and scraping and pulling on the doors, my voice worn to almost nothing. I spoke in gasping, hoarse whispers, over and over again, "Let me out. I want out. I need to fix this." My mind was running everywhere. All I could envision was my mother, Lila, my classmates, my teachers, Ricky the doorman, all of them suddenly feeling the intense pain of their hearts all slowing down, their breathing slowing down. I could feel the panic they must have felt, trying to figure it out, trying to draw a breath but not being able to move air fast enough to breathe in faster. The panic as they died from asphyxiation and blood pooling with no idea why this was suddenly happening and no one to hold them while it did because everyone else was dying too. Oh god, what had I done?

Something spoke to me. No, not spoke. It was inside my head, but not from me. Not a thought, but just there. It's hard to explain. There was just suddenly knowledge, in my brain, in a voice that wasn't mine, that said, "You overestimate yourself, child." I stopped beating the door. "You overestimate yourself and underestimate me."

I looked over at Dad, wondering what that not-voice was. Dad was laying prostrate, flat, belly on the ground, face down, trembling. OK. Should... should I being doing that? What... what was going on?

The word **CALM** came to me. Actually, the word seemed to just come through me, filling all of me. The ice and warm feeling when I used It was flooding through me, but not because I was doing or using It. And It was so much more powerful than I could ever have made It be. I relaxed. I didn't choose to relax, I just did.

My mind just knew again. "Do you think I would allow a power that I could not control? That I would not put safeguards on it to keep my creations safe? You OVERESTIMATE yourself."

Um, woah. OK, that kinda hurt a little. That knowledge was pushed into me hard and it felt like someone scraping the inside of me, the part of me that thinks and feels and knows. Not my brain, but that disembodied part of ourselves that is the inner monologue, the part that considers stuff and comes up with creativity. That part that is working when you say, 'Where'd that thought come from?' That part of me felt like it had just taken a punch.

"Get up." Yeah, not a question or command, I just stood up. "You did not destroy mankind." All right, yup, accepted as fact. I wiped my face, realized my hands were bleeding and rubbed at them. "You are forgiven this once. You did not know. Do not use your power on time again. Time is MINE to control. MINE! Return to your Trials. See them through." OK, will do, thanks. But I just wasted a buttload of time, I am probably going to fail now. The thoughts-not-thoughts sighed. I literally felt it sigh. "Fixed." I looked at the timer, it had stopped. Wait, huh? Doesn't stopped timer mean I failed? Inside my head somewhere I felt the whatever this was roll their eyes, or something like that. Does It have eyes to roll? I don't think It has eyes. Anyway, It was annoyed. "Lessers... The timer will resume, reset to the moment you left test five once you and your father have collected yourselves and are ready to resume. Go. Now." And It was gone. I felt It just be no longer in my head.

Dad must have felt It leave too, because he looked up. He looked completely awed. Instead of looking at me like I was the coolest thing since sliced bread (his norm because he loves his kid), or like I was some monster (the way he looked at me when I exited test five), now he was looking at me like he was scared of me, in awe of me, like how you might believe you would look at a unicorn. Very quickly, he stood up and tried to cover that and go back to the just looking at my cool kid face, but it only halfway worked.

"What was that?" I asked Dad.

Dad couldn't respond at first. His mouth worked, opening and closing but nothing was coming out. Finally, he got it together and said, "I've heard about it. There are rumors that Heka has talked to people before, but it has always been kind of an urban legend. You know, my friend's dog's girlfriend's step-brother on his mother's side worked with a guy whose girlfriend's dad talked to Heka, that type of thing. But never… my own daughter?"

I was confused, and told Dad so. "Who's Heka?"

Dad stared out into nothing. "Heka is It. Heka is the name of It. Not name, Heka is not a name. It is It. Every time we talked, Bella." Now Dad looked at me. "Every time we discussed the power, the glowing, the It, we were talking about Heka. The power that made everything in the universe, the substance even the gods don't understand? Heka."

Oh.

Wow.

"Heka wants you to finish the Trials," Dad said, still trying to shake the awe in his voice. He was almost there, but not quite.

"You heard It? I thought It was in my head," I asked.

"Not heard," Dad replied, a little bit more awe gone. "More felt. Imagine you and I were standing on opposite ends of a canyon and you yelled something. Your voice would echo through the canyon and I would get bits of what you said through the echoes. I wouldn't have heard you, per se. But felt the echoes. Because I was close enough to you when Heka spoke, I felt the echoes."

I shook my hands, trying to shake off the feeling of fear from the timer thing, and the residual woah from Heka. C'mon Bella, pull yourself together. I looked at the timer, *9:00:23:44:18.3*, and as I watched, it started counting down again. I guess Heka decided I was ready to start again. Who's gonna argue with the thing that made the universe? Not me.

"I guess I keep going then," I told Dad, pointing to the timer.

He looked and then nodded. "Ready?" he asked me.

"Not by a long shot," I said, kind of serious, kind of sarcastically. The final door on the right side creaked open. I walked over to it, took a breath and entered.

The first thing I looked at was the timer. *1:00:00:00:00.0*. One week again, OK phew. I read the plaque:

Test Six: Save the town.
Watch for birds.

Save the town, watch for birds. Either I got a fun little bird watching adventure, (ha, not likely) or I was saving the town from the birds. Shaking my hands again to loosen up, I stepped off the starting square.

Hey, I knew this town. This was the town from test two! Ben lived here.

The lights had come up with me directly in the center of town. People were bustling everywhere. The street seemed to be set up as a sort of farmers' market and everyone was milling around smelling apples and buying organic honey. I should find Ben, I thought.

I turned to the nearest stall, selling papaya juice, and asked them, "Could you tell me where Ben is." Crap, there could be tons of Bens running around and I didn't know his last name. But wait, the Ben that saved them from the snake would be pretty well known, right? I continued, "Where can I find the Ben that defeated the big snake?"

The stall owner looked at me like I had two heads just like the snakes. For a moment I was worried that, since each test resets when I am done, that this test city wouldn't know that test city, or that the test Ben from then wasn't this test Ben. But then the stall worker spoke. "Down the street, hang a left at the oranges. Three blocks, look for the sign with the dragon. Second floor."

Easy enough. I walked the way the worker told me. Right about the time I got to the oranges, a huge gong sounded. Everyone around me dove for cover. Under tables, in doorways, and windows slammed shut. I figured my wisest move was to follow suit and ran in a deep doorway. The door was closed already, so I just crouched in the doorway, and looked out towards the road to see what would happen.

The birds came, tons of them. They were swooping and swirling through the air. The birds were metallic colored, with copper-colored beaks. Everywhere they hit with their beaks tore open. Metal roofs had punch marks in them where the birds had pecked it. It seemed like the birds were molting. Feathers were flying everywhere. Not just coming loose and floating to the ground, but flying like someone threw a dart. And the feathers were sharp too. One landed near me and I picked it up. I sliced my thumb on the edge of it.

Above the flapping of wings and the people yelping, I heard a dog barking. Down the street, there was a dog being held back by a young man. The man was holding tightly to the dog's leash, pulling hard to try to get the dog to come inside with him, saying, "Fury, no! Bad dog. Bad! C'mon Fury, inside!" Hey, that's Ben! Found him.

As I watched Ben fight to get his dog to safety, I saw the dog try to bite the birds. He missed, but only because the birds seemed to give the dog a wide berth. Were the birds scared of the dog? Hm, I filed that info away for later.

Eventually, the swarm had passed through and a gong sounded again. People came out of their hidey holes and resumed their day like nothing even happened. What is it with these towns that just lived with murderous mythical beasties, got attacked and then just went back to life like it was nothing? Crazy.

"Ben!" I called out, waving my arms.

Ben followed the sound of his name, and saw me. "Bella!" He waved. "Stay there. Fury and I will come to you." Ben and Fury made their way through the crowds, slowly because apparently Fury demanded pets and head rubs from literally everyone. When Ben got to me, and gave me a hug, Fury must have decided that meant he had a right to demand of me too, and jumped up, putting his two large front paws on my shoulders and sticking his muzzle right in my face.

I laughed. I liked dogs. They are what humans should strive to be: kind, loyal, loving but hell if you mess with their family. And Fury was a wolfdog, I loved wolfdogs. "OK, OK," I told Fury. "You can have pets." I started petting the big dog and he jumped down off of me, laid down and rolled over, looking back at me with big soppy eyes. I knew a request for belly rubs when I saw it. I complied to Fury's request.

As I rubbed the belly of the dog, I looked back at the owner. "Tell me about the birds, Ben."

Ben got right to it. He knew from the bi-heads what I could do. "They showed up about a month ago. Mostly, they nest in the swampy area just outside of town. But they breed fast, so a few birds became a lot of birds became a swarm really quickly. Their beaks are copper and their feathers are metal and sharp. They can throw their feathers. Also, their poop is poisonous. Not venomous like the snake drool, just poisonous. Eat it or get it on your skin and you get sick. One of the doctors here figured out how to counteract the poison though, so if you start showing signs of that, he can treat it. It works like eighty per cent of the time, and people get better."

"And no one knows how to get them gone," I said, not asking.

Ben looked annoyed. "Yeah, pretty much. Stupid town. Oh no, a scary beastie, whatever shall we do? People are dying, someone should do something. Oh well, never mind, what should we make for dinner? Ugh." I knew I liked him.

All right. Info collected. Save the town from the murdery birds. Didn't need to kill the birdies, just get them gone. Birds didn't like dog. Dog liked to snap at birds. Would the oh-so-not-scary Fury that was currently a puddle in my tummy scratching hands be willing to hunt the birds, track them? Hmmm.

Ha! Got it. A plan. "Hey, Ben," I sing-songed. "Would you trust me to borrow Fury for a while?"

"You?" Ben gasped. "I'd trust you with my baby brother, my mother and anything else you could ask for. Why?"

"I got a plan, but involves your dog," I replied.

Ben handed Fury's leash over to me, rubbed the pup's head, and told him, "OK, Fury, listen to Bella and be a good dog." At 'good dog', Fury sat up and cocked his head to one side, as if listening to Ben. "Yes," Ben continued. "You can be a good dog when you want. Good dog." Then Ben moved away from Fury, stood up and looked at me. "Anything I can do?"

"Nope," I said. "Just your dog. Thanks. I'll bring him back soon as I can."

With that, I walked away with Fury, out of town and towards the swampy area Ben had said the birds nested in. When we were far enough away from people, I stopped.

"We need one more thing, Fury." I felt for my ice and warm. My Heka, I now knew It was called. I needed the hide from test one, in two pieces. One smaller one for Fury, one larger one for me. No weapon can penetrate the hide. Maybe the birds' beaks and feathers counted. And I needed rope or something to tie the hide to Fury's back.

A door plopped in front of me. I opened it and everything I asked for was there. I took the hides and rope out and the door popped away. I wrapped the smaller hide around Fury and secured it with the rope. Then I draped the larger hide over my shoulders. Fury waited patiently while I did this. Well, kind of patiently. He kept trying to lick me as I tied the rope around him. Then I took up his leash and we walked on to the edge of the swamp.

The closer we got to the birds' nesting ground, the more Fury began to pant and whine and pull on the leash. Finally, I gave up and let the leash go. Fury took off like a bolt of lightning, barking. Birds came out of the bushes in droves, diving and swarming. They would race in, darting at me and Fury, trying to peck us and throwing feathers. Then they would flee away as Fury chased them, snapping at any who got too close. He caught a bunch of them. Somehow, the feathers didn't cut the inside of his mouth as he chomped on the birds, killing them, then let them go. The birds that got caught in Fury's mouth all fell down after one quick chomp, dead.

I had pulled the hide over my head like a shield. The birds would hit it and bounce. It worked. It worked on Fury too. "Go Fury!" I yelled. "Get 'em, Fury!" I encouraged the dog to hunt the birds. The more Fury chased and chomped, the more disorganized the bird attacks seemed to get. He was laying them out, one by one. It was working.

But then Fury's rope loosened. The hide slipped sideways off his back. Fury had no idea, but the birds took full advantage of this opening. They dipped and whirled, avoiding his mouth. Coming up from behind, they threw feathers at Fury's unprotected back. Fury whirled, trying to grab the closest ones. He whined as each feather hit him.

Soon, Fury's back was a mess of protruding feathers. He had stopped attacking and was now lying down, whining and whimpering. Blood was streaming from each feather wound. No, oh no. Fury... poor puppy. As I looked on, the birds suddenly realized their predator had now become prey and were attacking him in force, pecking and throwing feathers and letting go their bowels all over him.

No. No! "Get away from him!" I yelled. "Go away! Go!" My voice reverberated in the air. The birds seemed to stop mid-flight. Then all at once, the swarms flew away. Away from Fury, away from the swamp, away from the town. All of them. They abandoned their nests in the bushes and took flight. The sky was black with the birds fleeing.

I noticed exactly none of this. I dropped my hide and ran to the dog. Fury was panting hard. "No, no, no!" I cried. "Oh, poor sweet Fury. Poor baby." Fury laid his head down on my lap. His breathing was labored.

He was going to die. "You can't die," I was crying hard now. "No, Fury. I'm sorry, no." I picked up the dog in my arms. The feathers sticking out of him scratched me everywhere. He was heavy. The poop the birds had dropped on him was rubbing into the scratches from the feathers on my arms and made them burn. I didn't care.

I ran. As hard and as fast as I could, the fastest I have ever run in my life. "Hold on, Fury," I said through my tears as I ran. "Hold on, baby. Don't die. You're a good dog. Good dog." As soon as I got close to town, I shouted, "Ben! Ben, help me! Ben. Anyone! Oh, please help."

Ben had been waiting near the edge of town and ran up to us as soon as he saw. He grabbed Fury from my arms and started running into town.

"I'm sorry, Ben!" I cried, as we ran. Ben turned here and there, pushing people out of his way, or if they didn't move fast enough, he mowed right over them. I followed him. My skin felt tingly and itchy. I ignored it. I would reset and be fine. I was not so sure Fury would. He wasn't supposed to be part of this game. I broke time in the last test. Could I break the rules and kill a dog? No, he won't die. He can't.

Ben reached where he was going and slammed through the door. There was an old man standing, and a young man sitting on a table. The old man was a doctor and the young man was his patient. The doctor, who had been examining something on the young man's skin looked up when Ben slammed the door open. The doctor pushed the patient out of the way. "Move!" he told the patient. Then to Ben he said, "Here, put him here."

"The birds are gone," I panted, still crying. "They are gone forever and this dog did it. He saved all of you. Save him, save him please." Then I curled up in a ball on the floor and cried. I didn't like hurting things. I really, really didn't. Humans have a basic goodness to them. And animals should be protected by us. No, I was not a vegan or anything. I ate meat because humans are designed to eat meat. But just because we have a predator-prey relationship and that relationship is good for the earth, doesn't mean I have to be hurtful. Humans are smart, we know how to end lives painlessly. We should, and many do, hunt and slaughter animals with kindness and compassion. And honor their sacrifice by using every part of them. Honor them. Honor each other. Humans are designed to be kind. Also, jealous and selfish, but we have developed brains! Use them to temper one nature in favor of the other. Be kind! And harming Fury was not kind, it was not good.

Ben handed Fury over to the doctor and stepped back. He watched the doctor for a bit then turned and noticed me. Ben knelt down and spoke, "I don't understand who you are. I just know that you show up when I need your help. And you help."

I looked at Ben, my eyes watery. He placed a hand on my shoulder and kept talking. "I also know that every time I see you, I also see red numbers. They just appear. The numbers count down. I saw you looking at the numbers a lot when we dealt with the snake. Are the numbers important to you somehow?"

I nodded and was about to explain the timer but Ben held up a hand to stop me. "I don't want to know. I think I probably shouldn't know. But if the numbers are counting down, and they are important to you, then do you need to do something before they get to zero?"

"Yes," I said weakly. "I fail otherwise."

"Did you do what you needed before they get to zero this time?" Ben asked. He was speaking gently to me, more gently than I felt I deserved.

I nodded yes. I thought I had.

"Then go," he said firmly. "Fury is in the best hands and there is nothing more you can do for him. Go, before your numbers run out and Fury's sacrifice is worthless. Go."

I realized I had no idea how much time was left on the timer. I could have failed already. Ben pulled me up, and pushed me. "Go," he said. "Go!" So, I went.

I ran back to the center of town. I had been in a blind haze following Ben to the doctor, so I didn't know where I was. I just kept following streets, running towards the people. The thicker the crowd, the more likely it led to the farmers' market.

There. I saw the plaque and the timer. I ran to it. The timer said *1:04:50:01.0*. I stepped firmly on the starting square. The door creaked open and I walked through. I had now successfully completed half the Trials.

When I came through the door, Dad took one look at my messy, blotchy face and the blood smeared all over me, and grabbed me, running his hands over me, looking for injuries. "Bella! What happened?"

I rubbed at the blood that was everywhere on me. "Not mine, Dad." The scratches had vanished, of course, and Dad knew the Trials would heal me, so I think he really just went into Dad-mode panic at so very much blood. "It's Fury's." Dad gave me a quizzical look. "Ben's dog, Fury is Ben's dog. I wasted time saving him. I had to, Dad. He helped me."

Dad cocked up one eyebrow questioningly. "Who's Ben?"

"Ben, Dad, Ben, the guy from the city in test six," I cried, frustrated with him. "The same city from the test with the however-many-headed snake. The city that sent Ben up to defend them from the snake until they could figure out how to kill it."

Dad shrugged. "Huh, the dude with the torch in test two has a name? Never knew…" Dad shrugged again. "Bella, the Trials run off the Heka, was made by it or with it or whatever. Think of it like a learning artificial intelligence. What you do in one test affects the tests further down the road."

Confused, I asked, "So the city in test six isn't the same city as in test two? They weren't both Ben?"

"They were the same city because *you* wanted them to be the same city," Dad explained. "The Trials learned that you wanted the tests to have some sort of connection between them, so it gave that to you. You thought it was the same city, so it was. You wanted to find Ben in that city, so you did." Dad let out a sigh that was part chuckle. "None of what is through those doors is real Bella, I thought you understood that. Ben isn't real. The dog isn't real. They all regenerate when you leave, resetting waiting for the next person to enter the Trials Arena and begin the tests their way." Dad laughed, "But that is so you, Bella. More concerned with a dog that regenerates the second you leave than with passing a test."

"How did I know he would?" I said accusatorily. "You never told me. You never told me it wasn't real people, real places. I didn't know that what I thought was living things in the tests weren't and that they would regenerate, that I would regenerate. I didn't know what I could bend, what I could break and what the hell I should leave alone." I was pointing at Dad, my finger inches from his face. "You never told me. You rushed me and rushed me and wouldn't listen to my questions. It was your job, Dad, yours, to prepare me. And you failed. Tell me this is the way it should be, with a person entering the Trials with no idea how they work at all. Tell me you didn't convince yourself that your daughter would be so talented, so perfect, that since she was yours, she would be so great she didn't need the warnings and the trainings. Tell me that's not true, Dad."

I kinda lost it. It had all been too much. The lion and the dog and the time inverting. And I was only half way done. I snapped. My chest was heaving as my breath came in raw and hot. I felt the Heka coursing through me, out of me, but I was so mad I didn't check It back.

Dad stepped back from me. I could tell it took a very big effort for him to step back. I was compelling him, but I didn't care. "Bella," he murmured. "Don't please, Bella. Don't compel me. Don't make me say it. I was wrong. I was wrong on so many levels. I should have done better to teach you first. But there was no time. They..." Dad groaned. He was fighting the compulsion. "Please, Bella. Not now. Not now, don't make me say it now."

Dad was hiding something. I knew it now. Something big and ugly. I could feel it. The Heka pouring out of me had latched onto his secret, his lie, and was twisting it, trying to pull it out of him. I wanted to know what the lie was. I had to know. But I had to complete the Trials. The Heka was pulling on that part of me too. Two different Hekas, or different parts or functions of It or whatever, were working in me at the same time. Get the lie out of Dad. Finish the Trials. Get the lie out of Dad. Finish the Trials. It was like tug-of-war with my insides. And Dad was in the middle trying to snap the end of the rope tied to him.

So, I let the Dad side go. Dad stumbled back, physically losing his balance after pulling so hard metaphysically. "I need to finish the Trials," I said, no less angry. "I need to finish, but after." I put a little compulsion back on Dad again, and it caught him off guard. "After, you tell me the lie." I let the compulsion go when Dad nodded his agreement.

I turned away from him. I had never been angry with my dad. Mad at him? Of course. I was a kid and he was my parent. Don't let me go to that concert two hours away at thirteen years old with only Lila's seventeen-year-old brother as adult supervision? Of course, I was mad at him even though it was the right, safe choice. Refuse to get me a puppy when I was nine? I was mad at him for a week. But angry? Bone deep, can I ever forgive you angry? No, not until now. Something told me that Dad had made a huge mistake with me, something that I would suffer because of for the rest my life. I felt it. His lie. Like a dark blackness in a place that should have been light.

I needed to put that anger away though. I needed to not feel it right now. Right now, I needed to finish the Trials. I looked down at myself.

And realized I had no shirt on. I took it off at the stables. I had been walking around all this time in only my bra. Oops. Ben had never said anything about my attire and neither had Dad, so I just forgot that my shirt was gone. Now there was blood and bird poo and dirt all over me. My hands were crusty with it all. There was soot from the stables, and I don't even want to know what else, streaked down my pants. I raised one arm, sniffed my armpits, and whew! I smelled.

Turning back to Dad, I saw he was pacing the floor, worried. "Dad," I said, trying very hard to be much kinder than I had been a few minutes ago. "Do you have any water? I'm kinda gross."

Dad looked at me. His face held questions. I knew those questions without him saying them. Are you still angry at me? Do you love me any more?

I looked back at him with the answers. Yes, I am still very mad. And of course, you're my dad. I will always love you.

Dad smiled and manifested two bottles of water out of his pocket. Yup, not gonna question that one right now, keep moving folks. Accept the Heka work and walk away. One bottle I poured over me, my hair, my face, my chest. I rubbed the water, scrubbing away the debris and stink as best as I could. Dad fished in his pocket again and gave me a towel and a shirt. I used the towel to wipe myself off and then put on the shirt. Then I drank the second bottle of water, rinsing my mouth out.

"Thanks," I told him.

Dad smiled, tentatively. We could fix this. Later we would fix this, I thought.

The timer was running. And the last door on the left, the one directly across from test six, had creaked open earlier while I was yelling at Dad.

I went through the door. The timer said I had a week for this task. The plaque was there, as always, saying:

Test Seven: Give him what he wants.
Do not kill him.

My mind wanted to ask questions but instead of asking any, I just stepped off the starting square, used to this arrangement by now. Farmlands came into view. Farms as far as the eye could see, in every direction. Were we in Kansas now?

There was a problem with the farms, though. I went into the field closest to me. It was growing potatoes. Half the potatoes were dug up and trampled. There was no rhyme or reason to the destruction, just potatoes tossed here and smashed there with no clear path to show where whatever had caused the damage had come from or where it went. I looked for the source of the damage and saw, at the other end of the field, a bull.

And not just any bull. A pure white, beautiful bull who looked really pissed off. The bull was running around, pawing the ground, digging and churning it. He would stop at one spot, stamp and blow, then run to another. This must have been the 'he' I needed to help.

How do you get a raging bull to tell you what it wants? Could I use my Heka on it? Part of me was afraid to try. Last time I used It on something I wasn't supposed to, I almost upended the world. But this was one bull, not time itself. If I did it wrong, the bull would just reset, right? I should try.

Gently, very gently, I pulled out my Heka and aimed for the bull. Tell me the truth, I urged, tell me what you want.

The bull stopped running. He snorted and pawed gently at the ground. An image came to my mind. Of course, the bull couldn't use words. Bulls don't talk.

In my head was the image of a sacrifice. I could see the priests and the carved stone alter with a statue of a man in front of it. On the altar, was a bull. A regular bull, not this pure white one. The bull was being sacrificed on an altar to some god or another, represented by the statue. The priest slit the bull's throat and its blood spilled down onto the statue. I could feel the god's displeasure at this. I could also feel the white bull's anger and frustration.

The images twisted and then righted itself again. Everything in the image had reset, except this time the bull on the altar was the white bull. As his throat was slit, I could feel the god's happiness and the bull's peace.

"You wanted to be sacrificed to a god, but the priest chose a different bull?" I asked the bull. He was all the way across the field from me, but he still heard me. The bull jumped and kicked. He pawed the ground and blew hot breath out his nostrils. I took this for a yes.

I can't kill the bull. The easiest solution to give the bull what it wanted was to find a temple and sacrifice the bull on the altar. But the rules said not to kill him. How do you sacrifice a bull without killing him?

While I thought, the bull went back to rampaging the field. My mind was blank. A sacrifice without death. Yes, sacrifice. No, death. What is a sacrifice? In what ways had I heard people talk about making sacrifices?

People had sacrificed their lives for causes. Monks set themselves on fire for freedom. Nope, death.

I paced back and forth. Sacrifices without death? A mother sacrifices her life to save her child. Death. A mother sacrifices her body to carry that child? Is that really a sacrifice? The right type of sacrifice, since the bull had intended on being sacrificed to a god not to children? Plus, bulls are boys and can't give birth to children.

Think. Sacrifices. Ugh.

Wait, didn't I read a story about Mother Theresa once that talked about her sacrifice? Yes. The story said Mother Theresa sacrificed her life to the good of humanity. She gave up worldly things, comfort and whatever, to help the poor and the sick. She sacrificed her life to this cause. Sacrifice but not death!

So, how does a bull who should have been killed as a sacrifice to its god sacrifice its life like Mother Theresa supposedly did? I stared at the bull for a while, watching him rip up potatoes and trample them.

What if I built an altar here? Dedicate it to his god and make him stay there. He could use his hooves to tear out any weeds that grew up by it. He could trample a path to the altar so people could go there to worship. He would sacrifice his life to the service of maintaining the grounds of the altar. Yes!

I ran across the field towards the bull, then cut a wide berth around him to the corner of the field. As I went by, the bull watched me and snuffed a lot. Please don't run me down, Mr Bull. I am trying to help. At the edge of the field was a spot where there were no crops. Things grew there, but nothing intentional. It was a wide swath of grass and stones and dirt between the potato field and the next field over that was growing corn.

Here, I ran around grabbing stones. In the center of the border land, I started piling them up. One stone at a time, I would dig it out of the ground and carry it to my pile. Then I would arrange the new stone with all the other stones in a way that felt good. I tried to make the pile look cool, but it ended up just a really tall pile of rocks. When I had as many good stones as I could find, I stepped back and admired my work. I was hot and sweaty again. There were a lot of stones and most of them were not light. Not a great pile, but definitely human made rather than nature.

Pulling ever so gently on my Heka again, I compelled the bull to come see what I made. The bull walked over. I stood very still when he came close. Please don't trample me, I thought again.

While the bull watched, I grabbed a thorn from a nearby bush. I pulled the thorn across my right pointer finger until the finger bled. I pushed on the skin, making more blood well up out of my finger. When I thought there was enough, I walked close to the pile of stones and spoke.

"Dear god of the bull." Hey, don't judge my prayers. I didn't know this god and had never offered up a real prayer before. Nothing more than please let me pass this test. "With this offering of blood, I dedicate this pile of stones to you and your worship. Hope you like it." I shook my finger so blood droplets flung onto the stones. "Here is this bull. He dedicates his life to maintaining the place for you. He will defend the stones from people who want to knock them down, from plants that want to grow on them, and will keep a nice path trampled down so that people can come here and worship you with ease. This white bull sacrifices his life to honor you and your worship stones."

I looked at the bull out of the corner of my eye. The beautiful white bull was not shifting and snorting any more. I turned toward the bull fully. "You have been sacrificed now. To this pile of stones that represents your god, your life has been sacrificed as a forever caretaker."

The bull ran from me. Aw, shoot. I thought I had failed and he was going back to rampaging. But then I watched where he was running. He was only running on the border land between the farms. He was stamping and churning the ground, but only in a straight line. Dude was building a path to the stones! Woo hoo! It worked.

I left the bull to do his duties, and walked back to the starting square. It had only taken me three days, sweet. Now the door would open, I thought. Nothing.

I finished the task. The bull wanted to be sacrificed and I sacrificed him but didn't kill him. So, the test was done.

Nothing.

"C'mon!" I yelled. I jumped up and down on the starting square. "It counts. It has to count. I bled on it and everything."

Nothing.

Was the bull not who I was supposed to have helped? Did I do all that work and wasted three days for nothing? I looked around to see what I could have missed. There wasn't another living thing for miles, just more farmland. Who else could it have been? I looked back at the bull. Did I miss something there? The bull was still running back and forth, making the beaten path through the grass. He looked happy. I swear, he looked like he was smiling. What more could he have wanted?

Maybe I missed something in the directions. I went to the plaque again and reread it. *Give him what he wants. Do not kill him.* Simple enough. The bull was male, so a he. I gave him what he wanted. I didn't kill him. If the bull wasn't the 'he', who was?

I looked at the timer. I had wasted half a day trying to get the stupid door to open. Even if I did figure out what I did wrong, I probably wouldn't have had time to fix it. I sat down on the starting square.

I gave up. I was going to fail this test. After all of that, I would fail and not even know how. Dad would be disappointed in me. Who knows what all sorts of trouble he caused bringing me here. There was something he wasn't saying, but somehow, I knew he had put it all on the line to do this. I was not sure what the 'all' that he had put on the line was, it was tied up in the lie he wouldn't let me compel him into admitting, but he had put it all out there. For me. Dad loved me. Dad sacrificed everything for me. He had been living in that heaven-like place, just working and enjoying life and he sacrificed it all to come to earth and make me, be my dad. And now I was going to fail him when it mattered most.

I looked down at the purple carpet under me and started picking at it. "I'm sorry, Dad," I said out loud, even though I knew he couldn't hear me. "I'm sorry. And whatever the lie is, I forgive you, OK? I forgive you and we will get through it. I love you, Dad."

The door creaked open. What the what? How did… What did I do? I apologized to Dad and forgave him and told him I loved him. Ohhhh. Dad was the 'he'. I had to give Dad what he wanted, my love and forgiveness. And not kill him. Sneaky, sneaky test playing family therapist.

I stepped out of the room. Dad was quietly waiting for me. "How'd it go?" he asked, much more subdued than any other time I exited a test.

"OK," I told him, avoiding his gaze. I don't know if I was going to tell him the solution for the seventh test or not. Right now, I wanted to just keep going. Do the next test and ignore how Dad was looking at me. The door to the eighth test creaked open. I didn't look at Dad as I walked over and entered the door.

Except for the stables, it seemed like the tests had a running theme of week-long time limits. This test did too. The plaque read:

Test Eight: Calm the mares.
Do not bleed while you do it.

OK, no bleeding while calming some horses. When I stepped off the starting square, the lights brightened on a stable. It was much smaller than the stable from test five, and way more ornate. The walls, roof and floor of the stables were made of copper. In the center of the stables was a pole made of gold. Tied to the gold pole with iron chains were four horses. The horses were mad.

No, not just mad, the horses were insane. You ever heard the saying 'I'm so mad, I could spit fire'? Yeah, these horses were that mad. They were literally spitting fire.

I walked closer to the horses, to examine them and see if I could figure out why they were mad. The horses were red, each a slightly different shade. Their manes were blood red and so were their tails. Their eyes were a burnt ember color and they were large and muscular for mares.

I tried probing them with the Heka like I did the bull but got nothing. I guess that trick only works once. The closer I got, the more the horses surged towards me. They were frothing and spitting fire, but the iron chains held them back.

The way the horses surged towards me made me think that getting free might have been what they wanted but it wouldn't necessarily have calmed them. In fact, it probably would have made things worse and most definitely would have made me bleed. A lot.

How to figure out how to calm the horses? I wandered to the back of the stables, giving the horses a wide berth. There was a door at the back of the stables and I wanted to see where it went. I opened the door and there was a soldier with his back to me. He must have been standing guard. Most people don't expect anyone to just walk through an invisible door in the middle of a room, so they watch the outside not the inside. I cleared my throat and the guard jumped.

"How did you get in here?" he demanded, pointing a sword at me.

"Yo, watch where you point that thing," I said casually. "I was let in."

"Who let you in?" The guard wasn't playing, and he didn't lower the sword.

"Never mind that now," I told him. Someone had once said if you act like you belong someplace, and are in charge, people will just let you in and follow your lead. I was trying that psychology trick on the guard. "Tell me about the horses."

The guard lowered his sword slightly. Progress. "The horses belong to the king."

I held up my hands, and wiggled my fingers in a gimme-gimme kind of way. "That's nice for the king. And?" I let myself sound impatient.

"They eat human and it makes them insane," the guard said as if it was just an everyday kind of fact.

"They what?" I was stunned. "Why?"

The guard shrugged. This was all old news to him, but he told me, "The king bought them as normal horses. He wanted them to be wild. So, he fed them human blood and did something, you know, weird." The guard waved his empty hand around indicating he was thinking weird meant magic or spells or something. "Then the horses became insane. They crave human blood and get super pissy when they don't have enough of it. Feed them humans, and they calm down a little but not for long."

What is wrong with this king? Dude, messed up. Feeding the horses human flesh made them calm down. From the way the guard said it though, it really just made them less crazy for a little bit, not really calm. I wanted to talk to this king. "Get him," I told the guard. When he looked like he didn't understand, I made myself clearer. "Get. The. King. Now. I want to talk to him."

The guard looked confused. It was a pretty ballsy move to order a king around. Oh well. Tasks to do, no time to waste. I gave the guard a super irritated look again and he scurried away, presumably to get the king. I wandered around the stables while I waited.

Soon, the door opened again and an older man swept into the room followed by the guard. He was in what looked to me like a very fancy bathrobe. It was red silk with a fur trim, and it flowed around him as he walked. Underneath the robe, he was wearing red silk pajamas. It must have been the middle of the night here, and I just ordered the king away from his beauty sleep. Not that sleep would have helped him much. He looked old and kind of scraggly. Even ignoring the obvious bedhead, his salt and pepper hair and beard were wild and obviously in need of a good trimming. "Who do you think you are coming into MY stables and demanding MY guard to wake me up and make ME come to YOU? No one demands of me!" the king bellowed.

"Um, yeah. I just did," I said as if the king's bellows meant nothing to me, which they didn't. "So get over it. What the hell did you do to these horses?"

The psychological trick of acting like you are in charge to make other people treat you like you are in charge only worked slightly on the king. Guess people who really are in charge are not so easily convinced. The king was not as quick as the guard to answer my questions. He only paused for a second before responding.

"Would you like a demonstration?" he growled. Yeah, pretty sure he meant he was going to feed me to the horses.

"Sure," I said casually. I was standing between the horses and the king. The guard was behind the king.

When I said yes to the demonstration, the king reached behind him, snagged the guard by his collar, and shoved him towards me, saying, "Deal with this insubordinate child!"

The guard stumbled as the king pushed him around. In his stumbling, he was reaching out for me, attempting to balance himself. He slid on the copper flooring. And I, seeing the geometry play out, took one giant step to the left. The guard slid by me, directly into the horses.

Who fed happily.

The king roared again, watching his guard be eaten. "You little…" The king stepped closer to me.

"Tell me how to fix the horses!" I roared back, adding just a hint of Heka for fun.

The king laughed. His laugh was a laugh of the deranged, high-pitched and maniacal. "You can't," he wheezed. "The only way to fix the horses, to make them not blood-thirsty any more, is for them to eat me. And who would dare feed their king to a horse?" He laughed more.

Thank you for that lovely piece of information. "You're not my king," I said, and grabbed the king's shirt. I pulled hard. The king tried to fight, but copper floors are really slippery. He was also only wearing slippers, so absolutely no traction added there either. Converse sneakers may not give the world's best grip, but they were way better than fuzzy slippers. He slid towards me easily.

I don't know how the king didn't have a perpetually sore throat if he was always yelling like that. He roared again, "You deranged, petulant infant! Get your hands off of me!" The king was close enough now to grab my shoulders. He clung to me with one hand and tried to pry my fingers off his shirt with his other.

Was I really just going to fling this guy into the man-eating horses? You bet. One, since he made them bad, it was his mess to clean up. Two, he would just reset when I walked out of the test. It wasn't murder if the death didn't stick.

The king and I wrestled around, both of us slipping and sliding on the floor. Sweat was dripping from both of us, just making the floor more slippery. The king reached out one hand, attempting to grab my face. He wanted to scratch my eyes out. Not only did I not like that idea because, ouch, but also scratching means bleeding and bleeding means I fail the test.

I put my hands in front of the king's and grabbed his wrists. I bent his arms backwards over his head, forcing him down to the ground. When he was on his knees, I stepped forward so I was standing over him. Then I pushed. The king was wearing silk pajamas. Silk on copper is worse than slippers on copper. The king slid across the floor, spinning around and around, just barely into the reach of one of the mares. The mare stretched out its neck and bit at the king's head. She got his hair between her teeth and pulled him closer to her.

The king was no longer roaring, but screaming. High-pitched waves of terror came off him as first one, then another, then all of the horses started to sniff and nibble on him. I turned away. I knew I should watch what I had done. If I could kill him that way, I should own it by watching, but I couldn't. I just couldn't.

Soon the screams died away and I looked back at the horses. They shook their heads and beat their tails as if swatting away flies. The red from their coats flew off like sparks and dissipated into the air. The magic wore off them and before me now stood four beautiful, black and gray mares.

The horses each nickered softly as I walked closer to them. Each one nuzzled me as I went by. I gave each one a pat on the nose and walked to the starting square. I wanted to free them, let them out. To run from this horrible place. But this was just a test. In a few seconds, I would leave. The test would reset and they would be horrible man-eaters again chained up in this room no matter what I did. So, I saved the time.

At the starting square, I saw that I had used just about five days. Cool enough. I looked at the starting square. "No funny business this time, OK?" And I stepped on. The door immediately creaked open and I walked into the hallway.

First thing I did in the hallway was check the timer. Since that whole thing with inverting time, I had been kind of afraid of the timers and not really paying attention to them super closely. Just checking if I finish each test in time or not. I thought it might be a good time to stop, take a breath, and see how well I was doing.

The timer read *6:6:16:34:40.4*. I had six weeks, six days, sixteen and a half hours and some change to finish four more tests. I had only used just over five weeks to complete the first eight. It was so weird, because if there had been no timers, I would have told you it was still that same Saturday I had entered the Trials Arena with Dad. Time didn't move in the tests except for on the timer. The sun didn't rise and set. It was always daytime. Heck, the woman with the deer said it was only a little past breakfast.

Maybe the Trials were lying to me. Maybe when we finished, and left this place, we would go back to Dad's condo and find that it was still Saturday.

So, what? I needed to not worry about how time worked here, or didn't. I had messed with that once and it went very badly. I wasn't going to do that again, so why did I care if it is still Saturday or November or a thousand years after I first came here? I didn't. All I cared about was that I was making good time on the tests. Almost seven weeks to finish four tests? I had time to take a little break.

Dad was waiting when I entered the hallway, but left me alone as I contemplated the timer. I turned to face him. "These tests are something else, man," I said to him.

"Yeah," he replied. I could tell he was still a little weird about our fight. I was too. We had never fought like that and I didn't know how to make up. I don't think he did either. So, we just ignored it happened and everything was a little awkward.

Dad pulled out a water out of his pocket for me. I took it and smiled. "Do your pockets of unusual sizes have something different? I am sick of water. If not, that's cool, but..." I plopped down on the floor and rested my back against one wall. I heard the door for test nine creak open, but ignored it.

"Pockets of unusual sizes..." Dad looked down at his pants pockets. "Oh! Funny. No. There's a fridge with snacks supplies and stuff behind the control panel on the wall. Coordinators and gods don't specifically need to eat, but it is still pleasurable. It's kept stocked up even though not many people use the arena any more. I have been grabbing stuff out of there when you are in each test, and putting it in my pocket so I can give it to you as soon as you want it."

A completely rational, non-Heka related answer. Huh. Why did I think his pockets were magic? Maybe because everything else here is, really. "Hm, well can you see if they got any sports drinks? Light blue or yellow, please. No red, yuck." I definitely would not be liking the color red any more. All the bad that I had seen? Blood and whatever else? I did not like red at all. I was even thinking that I would ask Dad to take down the *Visions in Red* painting in his living room when we went back home, even though I had always loved that one.

Dad opened the control panel, shuffled some things around, opened a second, smaller door and reached in. He pulled out a yellow drink and tossed it to me. "You want some pretzels or something while I'm in here?"

I nodded my head, "Gimme, gimme," I said, reaching out to him like a toddler.

He tossed a snack size bag of pretzels to me, grabbed a drink and pretzels for himself, then came over and sat next to me. "You are doing fantastic, Bella, just so you know," he told me.

"Yeah?" I asked with my mouth full.

"Yeah," he repeated. "I mean, we won't have the full results until we get the printout at the end, but your times? Fantastic!"

"Thanks, Dad," I said, then leaned my head back against the wall. I sat quietly for a bit, just drinking and eating my pretzels. I thought about all the tests. Lion hide, bi-headed snakes, a lost deer, a big boar... wait a minute... cleaning stables... I knew this pattern. Where did I know this pattern from? Birds, a bull, horses... Yes! I did know this pattern. I sat up straight. "Dad! I figured it out. I know what the tests are. They..."

"Bella, stop talking," Dad said quickly.

"But Dad," I tried again. "The tests, it makes so much sense. They..."

"Bella!" Dad said with more force this time. "Stop. Talking."

Suddenly, the door for test nine snapped shut. The four remaining doors shined brightly for a moment. When the shining went away, the doors were no longer dusty. Or wood. They were now gleaming blue, like they had just been painted. Test nine's door clicked loudly, open for me to enter.

"Um, what just happened?" I asked.

Dad groaned. "How did you know about the Trials of Hercules?"

"A class in school?" I said sheepishly.

"The one time," Dad said shaking his head. "The one time I want public education to fail you... Damn. Things you need to learn, do they teach them? Nooo, but things that screw you up later? Yep, all over that."

I looked at my father and raised one eyebrow. "Um, Dad? You all right?"

Dad groaned again. "You figured out the pattern. The tests change when you figure out the pattern. In training, you can choose any test of skill, faith, or ability any god, goddess, coordinator or human has ever done in real life. In an actual trial run, you get the Trials of Hercules, until you figure out that is what it is then they flip the game. Some people never figured it out. Some people took the Trials before Hercules took them, like me, so we had no idea because no one told that story yet. Actually, the Trials of Hercules myth is him doing this Trials Arena to be allowed to become a demi-god, just twisted a little through time. Once you finish the arena, you aren't supposed to tell anyone what the exact Trials are, but Herc has a big mouth. Now everyone knows them."

"OK," I said. "So the Trials change. How is that totally a bad thing? Do they get worse or more dangerous or something?"

"No," Dad replied. "Just different. Up 'til now, I knew what you came across in each of those rooms. I may not know how you solved it, but I knew what it was and knew how to worry and prep you. Now? I have no idea what is behind that door." Dad pointed to the ninth test door. "I have no idea how long you have to do it. I have no idea about any of it."

"So..." I said slowly. "Basically, your issue is you don't know when to start worrying about me?" I started laughing.

"Yes," Dad said pertly. "And that is very annoying."

I laid my head on Dad's shoulder, still giggling. "Oh my gosh, seriously?"

Dad and I just rested there for a while. It felt good to just stop and do nothing for a bit. But the timer was still ticking. An hour had passed, and I knew I needed to get up and get moving again. I stood up and brushed the pretzel crumbs from my hands on my jeans. My jeans were still seriously dirty. I wasn't sweating any more after my rest, but I probably stunk to high heaven. Well, maybe stunk back to common earth, since we technically were in heaven. Sort of. Anyway, I was nose blind to my own smell, and Dad hadn't said anything, so I figured no reason to care.

Dad got up and I looked at him. "Time to get back at it," I said.

Dad pulled me into a hug. "I love you, Bella Bella. Be careful."

"I will," I told him, and meant it. I was entering new territory, even for Dad. I walked to the door and went in.

The basic systems hadn't changed. There was a purple square of carpet bathed in light, with the rest of the room dark. There were the red lights of the timer, showing *1:00:00:00:00.0*, still one week. And there was the bronze plaque. I read it.

Test Nine (Modified): Meet me on the other side.

Modified. I wonder if the modification worked for me or against me in the scoring. I couldn't know until the end. So, I stepped off the starting square and the light bloomed to show I was on a river bank. On my side of the river, there was a lightly treed area behind me, not quite enough to be a forest but too thick to be random. The trees thinned out as the ground became sandier near the river bank. The beach area directly by the river was stony. In front of me was a wide river. Beyond that, on the other bank, was a full forest and it was hard to see through the dense trees. There was no beach type area on that side, only a small shelf from the water up to that land that showed how the water had eroded the sloping ground. Meet me on the other side? Probably the other side of the river. I had to cross the river.

The river looked wide, but that didn't mean it was deep. I picked up a stone from the shoreline and tossed it in the water. It plunked and sank. Hmm, didn't tell me much.

I tried again. This time I threw a long tree branch like a spear. I picked one off the ground that was about as tall as I was, slender but not too thin. It broke the surface of the water, sank fully and bobbed back up and floated away. The water was at least as deep as I was tall. And moving. The current had carried the stick away pretty quickly. I watched it flow away. In parts of the water, the stick twirled around before moving further downstream. So, not only was there a pretty healthy current, there were probably a bunch of large obstacles under the water that a swimmer could run into. Plus, there was no way to know what the undercurrent was.

On the plus side, nothing crazy came out of the water when I threw things in there. No alligators or crocodiles or mythical fish that eat humans. Still, I was never a great swimmer. Not good enough for an unknown body of water like this. And I was alone with no one to help me if I started to struggle.

Swimming across was out. I needed a boat. Too easy. Hello, Heka? I need a boat.

Hello? Boat, please.

"Hello?"

"Yeah?" Holy snot, there's someone there!

I looked up and down the shoreline and spotted them. Or well, their feet. There were two dirty, bare feet sticking out of a clump of bushes just south of me. I walked over to the feet and said, "Hello?" again.

"I said," a man sat up from the bushes. "Yeah? Whaddya want?" I looked the man over. He was about middle aged, and dark skinned. His skin was leathery, as if he had spent a lifetime in the sun. He was wearing denim overalls. Just denim overalls. No shirt, no shoes, nothing else that I could see. There was a flattened part of the grass under the bush where he had been laying. His voice did not entirely match his face. When he spoke, I thought he sounded more like an American southerner, but he looked more Middle Eastern. Oh well, globalized world and all that, people move everywhere from anywhere. "Can ya tell me whatcha want, or can I get back t' nappin?"

"I need to cross the river. Do you have a boat?" I asked. Maybe the door wouldn't give me a boat because I technically already had one.

"Uh, yup," the man said.

I waited, expecting him to produce the boat. He made no moves. "Can I borrow your boat?" I finally asked.

"Uh, nope," the man replied. "I's need it for work."

For work? What work? Sleeping? "What do you do?" I asked.

"I'm the ferryman," he replied.

For the love of all the Georges! He's the ferryman. That means his job is to ferry people across the river. Here I am telling him I need to get across and he is staring at me like I am stupid and he's the freaking ferryman.

Be nice, Bella. I knew that if I was mean or let my exasperation show, it would be harder to get the man to do what I wanted. "Well, then, can you take me across the river in your boat?"

"Uh, nope," he said.

"Why not?" I gritted my teeth and tried to remain calm.

"Uh, I don't wanna." The man seemed completely unfazed by how ridiculous this conversation was to me.

I huffed. "But isn't that your job? To take people across the river?"

The man shrugged. "Just because it's my job, don't mean I like it none."

Grrrrr. I looked up at the sky, composing myself so I could think. Up high, in the clear blue, there was some sort of large bird whirling around and around.

Think, I told myself. Myths with crossing rivers. The rest of the tests had been Herculean myths. Maybe this was some sort of myth as well. Of course! Greeks believed that when you die, you had to cross the river into the afterlife. But the ferryman would only take you across if you could pay! Maybe I needed to pay the man. But I didn't have any money.

"Hey," I said. The ferryman had laid back down to nap in the bush. He cocked one eye open when I called to him. "How much would you want to take me across the river? I could probably pay it." If I knew how much it cost, I could ask Heka to send it via door-mail.

"Uh, nah," the man said, closing his eye again. "Don't need no money just now."

I am a pretty patient person, but this man was wearing me thin. I didn't know if crossing the river was the only objective or just step one. The plaque said to meet 'me' across the river. Who was me? I tried again. "Is there anything you do need or want right now that I could trade for a ride across the river?"

"Uh, nope," he replied. "I just want me a nap." Oh, a nap? You want a nap? Well, you can trade me crossing the river for some dang peace and quiet, how about that?

I gently kicked the man's foot. "Dude, get up and take me across the river. I'm not playing."

The man's foot twitched, but mostly he ignored me. "Dude, get up! Get up now and take me across that river!" The guy was still silent.

"Screw this. Where's your boat?" I said more to myself than to him. I started poking around the bushes near the dozing man. His boat had to be nearby. "You won't let me borrow the boat, you won't do your job and take me, then I'll just steal your boat. What do you think of that, huh?"

"Good luck," the man chuckled without opening his eyes.

"What do you mean good luck?" I was getting tired of the games. 'Where is your boat?"

The man pointed to the river. I walked to the edge of the river and looked down. There underneath the water, completely sunken, was a two-man rowboat. For the love of cheese…

I put my hand on my forehead and looked back up at the sky for inspiration. The wheeling bird was still there, wheeling closer to the river. It was close enough that I could now tell it wasn't a bird. It was a man with bright white wings. Hm, maybe he could fly me across the river.

"Hey!" I yelled loudly up to the sky. I started waving my arms, trying to get the bird-man's attention. "Hey you up there! Can you help me? Can you come down and talk to me? I need some help."

The ferryman jumped up and grabbed my arm. "Just what do you think you are doin'?" he whispered irritably. "Why you callin' the bird-man down here? D'ya wanna get me in trouble?"

"Well, yeah," I answered him. "I mean, I didn't know the bird-man would get you in trouble, but you won't do your job and ferry me across the river. I need across. So, I figured flying dude could fly me across. If instead he kicks your butt and makes you do your job, all the same to me."

The ferryman looked at me, contemplating things. He didn't seem to be moving very quickly so I raised my hands again and yelled, "Mr Bird-man, I need across the river and the ferryman won't take me."

"Yes, I will," the ferryman stammered, then yelled louder at the sky. "Yes! Yes, I will. Silly girl course I'll take you cross the river. What's a ferryman's job but to take you cross the river?" The ferryman walked to the shoreline, still muttering and looking back and forth between the shore and the sky. "Stupid girl tryin' to get me fired. Tell you what, I shouldn't empty the boat all the way, let her get those little canvas shoes she gots all wet. Serves her right, who'd thought to use paintin boards to make shoes, anyhow."

I heard everything the ferryman was saying and smiled. While I watched, he picked up a tiny bit of string right on the edge of the water. As he pulled it, the water started bubbling. After pulling and pulling, the boat emerged from the water. I walked over to the boat and saw about six inches of water still at the bottom of the boat.

I crossed my arms, looked at the ferry man and cleared my throat very loudly. Then I looked at him and then looked at the water in the boat. The ferryman grumbled some more. "Stupid girlie thinks she's smart." He gave the string one more tug and the last of the water in the boat vanished.

The ferryman made a mock bow and held out his hand to me, sarcastically saying, "Your highness?" I took his offered hand, even if it was offered in jest, and stepped onto the boat. I sat at the back of the boat and waited patiently. The ferryman got in the front of the boat and reached over the bow. He looked like he was holding another string, but I couldn't see anything in his hands. He sat down facing away from me, towards the opposite shore and pulled on the invisible string.

The boat lurched forward. Every time the ferry man pulled on the nonexistent string, the boat lurched forward. By fits and spurts, we crossed the river. It took forever. For the first time in any test, I saw the sun was starting to set. I got nervous. How much time had this taken?

The boat lurched once more and bumped into the shore. We were across. Not wasting a second, I hopped out of the boat and scrambled up onto the shore. I started jogging down the shoreline, trying to figure out who I needed to meet there. The ferryman called out after me, "Hey, don' I get a tip?"

"Oh yeah!" I called back, not stopping. "Here's a tip: do your job the first time someone asks you to. You could have been napping again already if you hadn't spent so much time arguing with me!" I know, that was a little passive-aggressive.

I was looking all around me as I wandered the shoreline, looking for, well, anyone. But this random wandering was not going to help. I needed to be systematic in figuring out who I was supposed to meet on the other side. How could I be systematic when I had no idea who I was looking for or where I should be looking for them?

Start at the beginning. Of course, I should walk back down the shoreline to the same place the starting square was on the other side. From there I could fan out slowly, and find whoever was waiting for me. I sprinted down the beach, watching the opposite shore until I saw the starting square there. Then I looked around.

This side of the river was more wooded than the other side was. I looked into the trees and saw something glinting in the sunlight filtering through the canopy. I walked towards the glinting.

It was a bronze plaque. No way. Meet *me* on the other side. It wasn't saying I would meet somebody on the other side of the river. I would literally meet the plaque on the other side. I looked back across the river at the starting square. There was no stand with a plaque on it any more, and the timer was missing too. I walked closer to the plaque and saw the timer. It had been four days. I read the plaque.

Nice to see you again.

As I read those words, I heard the door creak open behind me. I went through the door and saw Dad standing by the door.

"So?" he asked.

"So," I replied. "No sweat. Just had to yell at a guy a bit." I smiled at him.

Dad looked at the timer. "You still have just over six weeks to complete three more tests. You are doing great, honey." He smiled. The now-blue door of test ten opened up.

I smiled back at him, "Then let's keep this ball rolling." I walked over to the tenth door and went through.

The timer said *1:00:00:00:00.0,* one week again. I read the plaque.

Test Ten (Modified): To pass, you must fail.
Do something.

To pass I must fail? How do I fail? I could get mortally wounded, Dad said that would make me fail. I could also run out of time. If I didn't complete the test in the time allotted, I failed. But what was the test I needed to complete? Did I need to fail? It also said, *Do something.*

So, to pass the test, I needed to do something, but also to pass, I needed to fail. Did I need to do nothing? For an entire week?

I stepped off the starting square, hoping the surrounding would make all this clearer. It was a late spring day in a rather dry desert with scrubby plants and not much else all the way to the horizon in every direction. Right in front of me, though, was a nice tree with big foliage that created a shady spot underneath it. On the ground beneath the tree, a blanket was spread out and there were plush pillows leant against the tree. It looked like the perfect place to have a picnic, or take a nice afternoon nap. Do something, but fail to pass. So, do nothing. That looked like a really comfortable place to do nothing.

I looked east, and the sun was just rising. I walked over to the blanket, fussed with the pillows and sat down. Once I was comfortably seated, I looked at the timer. It was rolling along as normal. So, I sat there. And sat there. The sun moved through the sky. When it got to its highest point, it got warm. A little too warm to be quite comfortable any more. I still sat on the blanket. The shadow the tree created moved across the blanket as the day went on. In the morning, the shade had been just to my right, not quite over the pillows but close. At midday, the shade was right over me and helped with the higher heat. By evening, the shade had moved to my left, leaving me slightly exposed to the setting sun again.

This felt wrong. I wasn't doing anything. So many tests had me running here and there. I kept having to think how to solve puzzles or save people or kill things that were unkillable. But now I was just sitting here with nothing to do. I watched as the sun made its way to the west and sank beneath the horizon. Then I watched the stars come out and streak across the sky. It really was beautiful, and felt good to just sit and watch it. At night, there was a small bit of a breeze which cooled me off from the warmer day. It made sitting there stargazing actually really pleasant. Even before all this stuff with Dad, I never really had time to just sit and watch nature.

The sun was rising in the east again. I looked at the timer. It had been one full day by the sun and one full day by the timer. So, I sat some more. The day moved on. Some animals came by for a visit. There was a bunny and a few squirrels. A butterfly landed on my knee. I wanted to pet them, but that would be doing something so I didn't. The sun set, the stars made their rounds and the sun rose again. I looked at the timer.

Two days down. The day was passing like normal when I saw a dust cloud moving towards me. As it got closer, I noticed there were people riding camels. That was what was making all the dust fly around. The camel riders rode right up to my blanket. Their riders dismounted and walked over, beating the dust from their clothes.

The first thing I noticed is that they were all my age. Three guys, three girls, all gorgeous. One boy, a blond with a perfect tan, spoke to me, "Hello AnnaBella." Oh my, was his voice just perfect, or what? "We have come all this way for you, AnnaBella. Would you come riding with us?"

Don't respond. To pass is to fail, do something. So, to pass I need to do nothing. Speaking is something. Don't do it. Don't even smile.

The matching set blonde girl tried. Together they looked like Barbie and Ken dolls. "Maybe you would prefer female company?" she said. Good on the test for not making hetero-normative assumptions, but no, thanks. I kept looking ahead.

Another guy walked up. He had a darker complexion, caramel skin with brown hair and eyes. My eyes instinctively darted to the girls. Yup, another matching set. Hey, I'll give the test credit. It is really with the times. No biases of any kind. If you wanted to try to appeal to someone sexually, you gotta make sure you tick all the boxes to hit their personal preference. Behind the second Barbie and Ken set was a third set, male and female alike, with very dark skin, black hair and very dark eyes. They hit all the boxes.

The sexy people were still talking, trying to convince me to go with them. I ignored them. What did they matter anyway? One, they were just part of the test and not real. None of them were actually interested in me. They were programmed to tempt anyone sitting under the tree to get up and go with them. They didn't even know me, so how could they want me? And two, even if they were real, or could be real, why did I need someone like that? I mean love and relationships are good. People should find someone to spend their life with. But it should be a partner, a helper. You should find someone who treats you good because they are good and you are good. They should encourage you to do better, and you encourage them. Would I get a relationship like that someday? Maybe, I didn't know. But for now, my goal was to pass these tests then go work with Dad.

I didn't need a relationship for that. Honestly, a relationship, even a close friendship would actually make doing the job harder. How do you look at a human you love and care about every day and know someday they will die and you will have to tell a god in a court all the bad things they ever did? Maybe that's why Mom and Dad had such a cold relationship. Because Dad didn't want to get too close, knowing he would have to be the prosecuting attorney at the trial of her life one day. He could get close to me because there was a chance I would never die, like him. But Mom? I could see how that would suck really bad and it would be better to not get so close to people emotionally like that.

It made me very glad that Lila was going to college so far away. I wouldn't have to make the choice to either cut her off, and maybe hurt her in the process, or stay close friends and hurt myself when I had to be the lawyer at her afterlife trial. She had always been a good friend to me. Since we met in third grade, we had been two peas in a pod, me and Lila. I wouldn't want to do anything that made her sad. But I also would have had a hard time staying her friend, being supportive of her, and never being able to say to her, "Hey, you may not want to do that thing you are thinking of doing because the god of your religion will definitely hold it against you when you die. I know because I will have to tell them about it." Cutting myself off from a friend like Lila would be the best way if I was going to follow in Dad's footsteps.

Could I really make that choice? Cut myself off from everyone? I closed my eyes and just sat with that idea for a while. Yes, I think I could. Dad seemed happy with his life, and we would have each other. Yes. I opened my eyes, at peace with that thought. I am fine by myself.

The Barbie and Ken doll sets of humans had walked away to a nearby tree and sat in the shade. I could hear them talking but could not quite make out the words. The sun was setting and I didn't care. The stars whizzed by and night turned to day. Day three in the books.

Day four passed uneventfully. The Barbies and Kens stayed under their tree, sleeping and talking, but I paid them no mind. I was actually kind of happy sitting here doing nothing. The days were getting a little warmer, and I was sweating a little during the hottest part of the day. But I am not human, not all the way, so I won't dehydrate or overheat. The days can pass and I will be fine.

Day five, there was a huge rolling cloud of dust coming towards me fast. I took a deep breath and let it out. The Barbies were freaking out. I just sat there. The horde causing the dust storm finally arrived. It was soldiers. Lots of soldiers brandishing swords and screaming in a language I didn't know. They started running around me, whipping their swords near me, acting like they were going to stab me.

I internally smiled. They would not scare me. They had two options. They could kill me or not. If they didn't actually kill me, they were a useless threat not worth getting worked up over. If they killed me, I failed the test and regenerated in the hallway. If the point of this test was actually to fail, then I would have passed earlier than the full seven days and I could thank them for saving me time. If I was wrong, and misinterpreted the test, then I failed for real. But I was willing to take that risk and sit here, doing nothing, believing that failing by doing nothing was passing by not doing something. So, I really wasn't adding any more risk by dying early. I trusted that my answer to the plaque's riddle was right and I would see this out. I closed my eyes and just relaxed. The soldiers could brandish swords all they wanted.

Day five passed away and the soldiers stopped riding around and playing with their swords. They went a distance away and stayed there, jockeying their camels and doing not much else. Day six came and went quietly.

Day seven started and I was feeling good. Almost done. There was a tiny dust cloud in the distance. It was one man on a camel riding towards me. The camel stopped right by the blanket and the man got down, beating dust from his clothing. His back was to me. The man turned around.

Dad? Wait, don't say it out loud! The man on the camel was my dad. But he couldn't be. How was Dad in the test? Was that one of the 'modified' things or was Dad always in this test at this time? Or was this one of those times where the test reprogrammed itself to what I wanted, like it did with Ben?

Dad walked over and knelt down next to me. "Bella, what are you doing? You need to get up and finish the test." No Dad, the test is to do nothing. I am doing the test. "Bella, do you want to fail?" Yes. Well, no but yes. Failing is passing, Dad. I wish I could answer you but that would be doing something.

Dad walked around a bit then came back over to me. He knelt down and spoke again. "AnnaBella, you need to get up." No, Dad. Dad threw his hands up in the air, exasperated. "Fine Bella, I give up. You don't want this? Why didn't you just say so? Just get up and we can go home." Nope, nope.

Dad walked to the edge of the blanket, his back to me and spoke again. "You want to know the lie, Bella? That lie you almost had out of me after test six?" How did the test know about what happened in the hallway? I really didn't like this. "The lie is, Bella, you are not worth this." Dad turned around and looked at me. "You're not. All that time. All those years planning, all that time with that stupid, sniveling human you call a mom, and for what? For this." He gestured to me. "This lump of subpar nothingness. The lie is I want to go home. Not the condo, but my real home, without you. I don't care to ever see you again because you were not worth it."

No. This was not my dad. Not really. I closed my eyes, but I could still hear him, droning on and on, pointing out every one of my faults. He even knew the mistakes I made in the other tests that wasted time. My eyes were stinging like I might cry. You can't cry! Stop it! Crying was doing something and that non-thing, that not-my-dad was not worth it. He wasn't real. He was a part of the test. Just like the Barbies, just like the soldiers. His opinion didn't matter.

I took a really deep breath and blew it out slowly. Plus, even if it was Dad for real, did his opinion matter at this point? This was a twelve-week test that I was finishing, if the schedule held, with about four weeks to spare. That had to be some sort of impressive. And even if it wasn't impressive to the immortal crowd Dad ran with, just passing would be cool to the human crowd. And outside the tests, I was still pretty kick ass. I had a 3.7 GPA in high school, not too shabby. I was in the Honors Society. I volunteered with different places all the time. I read a lot and watched the news. I was ready to be active in politics when the time came, or at least be a smart voter. I was worth something to me. And that was what mattered.

The more I thought that over and over, the quieter Dad's voice got. Eventually, either he had stopped talking or I was so at peace with myself, I had stopped listening. A loud buzz sounded and I opened my eyes. The timer was at *0:00.0*. Time had run out and the door opened.

I stood up to leave, feeling really good. Well, except for the pins and needles in my legs, yikes! I shook it off and walked to the door to my real, and really frantic, dad.

"Bella, what happened?" he asked. "You were in there for a whole week. No test is longer than a week. Are you OK, did you fail?"

I smiled really big and pointed to the hallway timer, which was still ticking down. "Nope, I passed."

"What?" Dad asked, really confused.

"To pass, you must fail," I repeated. "I let the timer run out and did nothing."

Dad hugged me tight. "You beautiful, smart child," he said. He held me and rocked me back and forth. It felt so good after the fake dad saying all those mean things, and I found myself fighting the urge to cry. That was not the lie, that he didn't like the daughter he had made. I didn't know what the lie was, but it wasn't that.

The door to the eleventh test had creaked open and Dad let me go. "You have five weeks, one day, two hours, fifty-six minutes and twenty-three seconds left.

If you hurry, you may just break the record for the fastest Trials. Go," he told me.

I grabbed Dad one more time for a quick hug, wiped my leaky eyes, then went in the door.

Through the door for test eleven, the timer said one week and the plaque said:

Test Eleven (Modified): Eat the apple.

I stepped off the starting square, into the light and found myself in a garden. There were trees around me, but not ones that looked like forest trees. The trees were growing in very straight rows that didn't happen in nature. This was someone's orchard. I walked around the trees nearest to me. They were apple trees.

Was it just me or were the tests getting easier? I reached up my hand to grab an apple from the tree.

A man spoke. "I really wouldn't do that," he said casually.

I followed the sound of the voice. He was at the edge of the orchard, leaning against a large wall. The man was young, but not too young, maybe my dad's age, and beautiful. He had long blond hair and a close shaved blond beard. His hair was slicked back from his face and tied into a ponytail about halfway down his back. He was also very tall. The man was eating an apple.

"Why not?" I asked, "Do you own the orchard?"

The man took another bite of his apple, chewed it slowly, then answered, "No, but I know who does and she won't be happy if you try to steal from her."

"You know the owner?" I asked the man. "Can you show me where she is so I can ask her to give me, or maybe sell me, an apple?"

The man took another bite of his apple. "These apples aren't for sale," he said with a full mouth.

"OK, if the owner of the apples won't let me steal one, be given one, or buy one, can I have a bite of yours?" I asked.

The man took a bite of his apple again, looked me straight in the face, chewed slowly, then took another bite. "Nope," he said, his mouth stuffed with apple. "Because I ate it all." He took one more big bite, thew the apple over the wall and then grinned. Bits of apple fell out of his over-stuffed mouth.

Ew, gross. A not-so-nice part of me hoped the guy choked on the apple. The bigger part of me realized that was not cool to think. He was a jerk, kind of, but it was his apple.

"There is a way," the man said after he swallowed all the apple in his mouth. "Maybe I could help you get an apple." The man stood up and walked closer to me. When he got close, I could see that he really was very beautiful. His skin was flawless. And was he wearing cologne?

"How could you help?" I asked, glad I had bit back being mean earlier. See? Being mean would have made him not help me. Always be nice.

"I said maybe I could." OK, that time when he said it, his voice sounded a lot slicker. Like maybe this wasn't the best guy to be trusting. The man had kept talking. "So, I am a shapeshifter, you know. I can change into anything I want. Even was a horse once…" Not man-eating, I hoped. "The lady who owns the apples, when she picks them, she puts them in a special box so only the people who she likes can get them. The box is made out of wood, ash wood."

I waited. Was there more to this plan? Was he done talking? An ash box containing the apples and a shapeshifter, hmmm. The man was staring at me. He kept raising his eyebrows and gesturing to me, as if he expected me to figure out where he was going with all this. I'll admit, I was stumped.

The man finally leaned down and whispered out of the side of his mouth, "Ask me to turn into an emerald ash…"

Ohhh. I interrupted the man, thinking I had figured out his plan. "Emerald ash borer. Can you turn into that bug and eat through the lady's box to steal me an apple?"

The man put his hands in his pockets, wandered around for a minute as if he was thinking. "I could. I mean, that would be so simple for me to do. But why should I?"

"It was your plan," I said incredulously. I mean, he thought of it, he offered it up to me. Now he was not sure.

"Yeah," he turned the oil back on in his voice. "But I don't need an apple. I just had three. I pitched the leftovers over that wall." The man pointed to the spot where he had been leaning against the wall. "So, why should I steal an apple I don't want for a little girl I don't know? What is in it for me?"

I sighed. Don't call me a little girl. "Can we just… make this easy and you tell me what you want?" I asked.

The man smiled very wide. Something in my gut did not trust that smile. "I want to go with you," he proposed.

Go with me? "Go with me where?" I inquired.

"Back through the door," he responded. "You came in through a door that disappeared after you walked through it. I assume, after you eat the apple you so desperately want, the door will reappear and you will leave that same way. Take me with you." The man smiled even more now.

I thought about this. "You turn into an ash bore beetle. You eat through the owner lady's box," I stated out each step very carefully making sure this man was not going to trip me up over some part of what we were agreeing to. "Until an apple falls out of it. I grab the apple, eat it, and you and I go through the door when it opens. That's it?"

The man spread his hands wide, still smiling. "That's it." He reached out one hand to me. "Deal?"

I shook his hand. "Deal." I was still shaking his hand when he transformed into a tiny beetle and flew away. I had to run to follow him. Somehow, I could still see him as we went along. Emerald ash borers are usually tiny, smaller than a penny. Maybe as a shapeshifter, the man allowed himself to stay big enough for me to follow until he got to where we were going. We ran/flew through the orchard and came out at a cottage. Outside the cottage, amidst a garden of wildflowers, there was a young, beautiful woman. She was walking through the garden, sniffing flowers and it seemed like just generally enjoying being outside. On her right arm hung a box. The box was made of ash wood branches cut to equal lengths and lashed together to make six equal parts: four sides, a top and bottom. The box had a leather strap on top that the woman used to carry the box like a purse.

The man-beetle flew into the garden. I stopped at the edge of the garden and hid behind a birdbath. The man-beetle landed on the box. He was small, too small for me to see any more so probably the right size for the beetle he was shaped like, and I couldn't see exactly what he was doing, but pieces of the ash branches making one side of the box started falling away.

Soon, there was a hole large enough for an apple to fall through. The woman bent over to pick a flower and when she stood back up, two apples came tumbling out of the hole. The woman seemed not to notice. She walked to another part of the garden, unaware she had lost the apples.

I ran to the apples. I tried to be quiet but quick, dipping behind tall plants or garden ornaments so she wouldn't see me if she turned around. I grabbed one of the apples and high-tailed it out of there, back through the orchard.

Once I got back to the spot where I first saw the man, I stopped and took a huge bite of the apple. Oh my goodness! I am not the biggest fan of apples, but man! The apple was crisp and sweet and juicy. The flavor was just perfect. I ate it all down to the core.

The man sauntered back to me, still grinning like the cat who got the cream. "Good, huh?" he chortled. I nodded and he continued speaking. "Ready to go?"

I nodded and wiped my face. The apple juices had dripped everywhere on me. "Yeah, back through the door," I told him, pointing to where the timer and starting square was.

We walked over and I glanced at the timer. Only used three days, cool. The man and I stepped on the starting square and I waited. Nothing happened.

Oh no, not this again. The man chuckled under his breath. "Problem?"

"It isn't opening," I said confused. "I finish the task, step on the square and the door opens. But it's not opening. I don't understand, I ate the apple."

The man seemed like he couldn't hold back laughing, but was really, really trying. He walked over to the plaque and asked, "What's this? The rules?"

"Yeah," I replied, "I read it at the start to know what I need to do." I walked over to the plaque and stood next to him. "It just says to eat the…" I looked at the plaque. The words had changed.

Test Eleven (Modified): Eat the apple.
No one may leave the testing area except the one on trial.

Crap. The man couldn't leave with me. Did that mean our deal was broken? Did the apple I ate not count?

As I thought this, something began to tickle the back of my throat. I coughed. The man looked at me. He was still giggling. I coughed harder. The tickle got worse. The man started laughing harder. I felt like I was choking. I coughed and coughed and coughed. Bent over double from coughing so hard, I got scared. I couldn't breathe. How do you do the Heimlich on yourself? I started panicking because I couldn't remember. The man did nothing but watch all of this and laugh.

One more hard cough and something flew out of my mouth and thumped on the ground. It was the apple, whole and perfect like I had never bitten it.

As I was struggling to catch my breath, the man was full out laughing. "Every time," he cried from laughing so hard. "Every time, you guys fall for it."

"What?" I wheezed. My throat was on fire.

The man put his hands in his pockets again and started slowly meandering away. "Every time one of you comes through that invisible door, you are so desperate for an apple. It's fun to watch you squirm and squeal and get angry when you realize the deal you made was completely invalid. You have no power over the door. You just wasted a whole bunch of time on a promise you couldn't keep." The man laughed deep and loud now. "Good luck getting another apple." Then he walked away, talking to himself. "Ah, love that. Breaks up the boring day."

He... I... WHAT? That man, I growled, "Goddamnit! I hope you choke, you... you... UGH!" Three days! I wasted three whole days on an oily, slimy trickster who was just doing this for kicks. That rotten... Bella! Get ahold of yourself, I thought. I didn't have time to waste hating that guy. I needed to eat an apple.

I went back to the orchard. The man said not to steal the apples, but was he just toying with me? So, maybe it was just that simple. Pick one, eat it. I reached up to grab a low-hanging apple from the tree.

As soon as my fingers brushed the apple, it disappeared. Dang. Not that easy.

I had to think. How could I eat an apple I couldn't pick from the tree? Maybe the lady would just give me one? Nah, I'm sure by now she noticed the hole in her basket. Even if she was nice and would have been willing to share before, I bet Mr Slick Guy already told her I tried to steal from her through that hole. Couldn't waste time trying that. Who knows what kind of complications it would have brought.

Think, Bella. Most tricksters use some truth in what they say. It's how they trick you into believing them. What had the man said? He said he had eaten three apples already. And how did we know that was true? He was eating one when we walked up. Then he threw the core over the wall. No. Not the core. The rest of the apple. There was probably still a lot of fruit left when he threw it over the wall. He just said it was all gone to tick me off. There was at least a quarter of uneaten apple behind the wall. Maybe more if the guy was just as wasteful with the other two apples.

I ran to the wall. It looked easy enough to climb. Rough stones cut into square bricks with wide mortar joints that work great for hand and footholds. Not too tall, just about a foot over my head. Easy to jump down on the other side. As long as there wasn't anything super dangerous, or someone plastered over the other side of the wall, I should be able to drop down, grab the apple bits and come right back.

I started climbing the walls. It didn't take long for my head to be over the top. I paused and looked around. Empty fields. It didn't look so bad. No raging fires, or scary beasties running around. I climbed higher, swung my legs over and sat on top of the wall. I looked down at the ground beneath me. Seemed normal. And there were three apple cores right there below me.

Feeling a little untrusting, (hmm, wonder why?), I took some small pebbles from the top of the wall and tossed them onto the ground next to the apple cores. Nothing happened. I flipped over onto my belly, placed my hands on the wall, and gently started to lower myself down. Eventually, I was hanging by my hands, my feet only a few inches or so from the ground. I let go.

My feet touched the ground and I braced myself, looking around. Nothing happened. Quickly, I grabbed the three apple cores, stuffed them in my pockets and climbed back up the wall. I dropped down from the top, and took my prize to the starting square.

Once there, I pulled the biggest apple core out of my pocket and took a healthy bite, staring the entire time at the plaque. I chewed, swallowed and waited. The plaque shimmered a bit, then changed again.

Test Eleven (Modified): Eat the apple.
No one may leave the testing area except the one on trial.
To complete the test, the full weight of one average apple must be consumed.

"Cheater!" I yelled at the plaque. "You're changing the rules!" The plaque did not respond to my outburst.

OK, yelling at a plaque would not help me finish the test. I needed to think again. The full weight of an apple needed to be eaten. The full weight. I pulled the other two apple cores out of my pocket and looked at all three. Together, they probably made a full apple. But how to eat them? They were mostly just core. The weight of one apple needed to be eaten.

But not necessarily in the form of an apple. I called the Heka. I need a mortar and pestle, quick! A door plopped down. I opened the door and pulled out a granite bowl with a matching small, thick stubby stick. The door popped away. On the starting square, I sat down and put the cores into the bowl. Then I beat the cores with the stubby stick, the pestle, as hard and as fast as I could. I kept one eye on the timer as I worked.

The hard cores quickly became a thick paste under my beatings. Once it was a stirable consistency, I tossed aside the pestle, and began shoveling handfuls of the paste into my mouth. I ate it, seeds and all, one eye on the timer, one eye on the plaque. It was gross and bitter and I gagged. But I swallowed it. Handful after handful, scoop, put the mush in my mouth, swallow. I had finished the majority of the bowl and was just about to start licking the mortar when I heard the door creak open. I dropped the bowl and exited the test, with only one day remaining.

In the hallway, Dad was uber excited. "Bella!" he exclaimed. "If you can get the next test done in two days, you will beat the fastest time through the Trials ever." He didn't give me a chance to think or breathe, but pushed me to the twelfth and final door, which was located directly across from the first test door. The door clicked open, and he pushed me. "Go, go, go, go, go."

I turned as he was nudging me toward the last test door, and tried reaching into Dad's pocket. When he felt what I was doing, he reached into his pocket himself and pulled out a blue sports drink. He shoved it into my hands with one hand and pushed me towards the test door with the other. "Here, go, go," he said.

I took a quick swig, hoping to get rid of the bitter taste in my mouth. Unfortunately, the blue drink and the bitter apples did not mix well, like orange juice and toothpaste. I spit it out, tossed the bottle back to Dad and walked through the door, smiling. I could still taste the bitter apple sauce I had made. But Dad was so excited and he thought I could break some records. Let's go for it, Dad, I thought.

I had a week by the timer, but only wanted to use two days. I read the plaque.

Test Twelve: Go to Hell.

Hey, rude. Wait, this test didn't say modified. I was back to the Herc stuff, I thought. What was that last test? The three-headed dog guarding the entrance to Hell. He was vicious but slept when music played. The test wasn't being rude. It literally wanted me to go to Hell.

I stepped off the starting square, feeling very prepared. There it was, just like I thought. Huge three-headed dog? Like big as a house huge? Check. Very angry? Check. The dog was growling at me from all three of its heads. Tiny little trapdoor under its belly? Also, check. Now I just had to make the dog fall asleep and go through the trapdoor. Easy. I needed music.

Thank you, the wonders of technology. I called on the Heka and asked for an iPod loaded with a three-headed dog preferred playlist and a multiple user wireless earbuds. The door plopped down and I opened it. One music player, not the brand requested, and two sets of Bluetooth earbuds. OK, good enough. I grabbed the tech and the door popped away.

The music player was loaded with a bunch of random songs. I pushed shuffle-play and turned the volume up as loud as it would go. Pop music started blasting out.

I watched the dog. All three heads started bopping along with the music. They were no longer growling, but definitely not falling asleep. In fact, their singular butt started wiggling like they were dancing.

Not a good song choice. The dog liked it but it wasn't falling asleep or getting out of my way. I pushed the shuffle button again and hard rock blared out. The dog loved this song, I could tell. One head was head banging. Another was swaying back and forth. The third moving its lips as if attempting to sing along. Still not sleeping.

I hit the shuffle button again and the lip-syncing head snapped at me. I jumped back a bit. "OK, OK, I'll put it back," I told the dog. I pushed the button for the player to backtrack and the hard rock song came back on. The dog settled and all three heads picked up the beat again.

It wasn't a bad song. Not the screamy death rock that you couldn't understand what they were saying, but a cool, classic rock with more punch. I sat on the floor cross-legged with the player in one hand and the earbuds next to me. Waiting impatiently, I couldn't do anything but lip-sync along with dog head three.

The song ended and the music player shuffled the list again, making a beautiful ballad come on. The dog's heads started to sink to the floor. One head rested on a front paw. The second leaned against the first head. The third laid down on the other front paw. All three started snoring. Emotional ballads. Got it. While the song continued to play, I searched a ballads playlist. When the song ended, before another one could start, I switched to the new playlist and hit shuffle-play.

The dog kept sleeping. I carefully walked over and looked for the trapdoor. Shoot. The trapdoor to Hell was under the third head and the paw that head was resting on. I gently grabbed the paw and tried to move it out of the way. The thing was heavy. I pulled and pushed. It didn't budge. I strained as hard as I could, bracing one foot against the closest wall for leverage. Nothing.

I would have to wake up the dog and make it move off the trapdoor. Then, I would have to make it fall asleep again and hope it didn't land the same way again. That sounded risky. How many times would the dog fall asleep on top of the trapdoor before I got it where I wanted it?

Then I realized, I didn't have to wake up the whole dog. Just the one head. I walked back over to the tech on the floor and picked up the two sets of earbuds. Slowly, I walked back over and climbed up the dog's haunches until I could sit on top of the first head. Ever so gently, I place one earbud in the right ear and one ear bud in the left. I flipped the dog's floppy ears back and forth to make sure the headphones wouldn't slip out if the dog moved that head some. Then, I carefully crawled across the dog's shoulders to the second head and repeated the process. I climbed back off the dog, went over to the music player and turned on the Bluetooth. There was a moment of quiet while the Bluetooth connected to the earbuds. All three dog heads stirred. C'mon, c'mon.

The first and second dog head started to relax again. The earbuds must have connected. The third head, hearing no music, woke up and started growling. He cut himself off mid-growl, though, and looked around confused. 'Why were the other two heads still asleep?' I could almost hear him thinking. From his angle, he wasn't able to see the earbuds. Head three growled some, but softer than before when he had backup. The dog had no clue what to do without its twins.

"Hey, buddy," I said softly. The third head growled softly, so softly that it almost turned into a regular bark. "Hey, good puppy. Good puppy." I kept softly saying nice things to the dog while slowly stepping closer and closer. "Who's a pretty boy? Yeah, you are. Such a pretty boy. You want lovins? Want a head scratch? When's the last time anyone gave you a good head scratch, Cerby?"

The dog seemed intrigued by what I was saying. The growls had settled into little woofs and snuffs. At the word 'scratch', he had cocked his head to one side. "Arf?" he barked, questioningly.

"Yeah, boy. Don't eat me and I will give you lots of scratches," I told him, stepping closer and closer. The dog lowered his head closer to the floor. I stole a peek at the other two heads. Still asleep and this guy looked like he would love some attention. Gently, I reached out and just barely touched the side of the dog's head.

At that touch, both of us pulled back in fright. Then we stared at each other, sizing one another up. Slowly, even more slowly, I reached my hand back toward his face, while he leaned in towards my hand. This time, neither of us jumped back at contact and I began to pet the third head of Cerberus. The dog closed his eyes and growled in his throat.

It wasn't the 'I want to eat you' growls from before, but more of a 'this feels amazing' growl, so I kept petting him. The dog turned his face so I could reach more around his ear. I scratched there for him really well and he seemed to love it. Aw, poor monstrous puppy. Has anyone ever loved you?

Cerberus lifted his head so quickly, it knocked me off balance. Panic rose up in me. Was he over this game? A quick look told me no, he wanted his chin scratched now. Petting the mythical three-headed guard dog of the underworld was fun, but I had to remember my main objective. Get to the trapdoor.

I looked at the floor. The trapdoor was right there. The huge paw had slid off and it was mine for the taking. I reached up and scratched the third head's chin, moving my way down its neck to cover the fact that I was walking towards the trapdoor. Cerberus's back right leg was thumping on the floor. I had hit that puppy spot that triggers the scratch reflex.

Aw, cute. Bye!

I had reached the trapdoor, thrown it open and jumped in before Cerberus's leg stopped thumping. I was falling down a shaft, with the third head barking after me. The earbuds must have fallen out because I heard all three heads start barking. It seemed like I was falling for a while.

I looked down and there was a square of light growing beneath me. Brace for impact, I thought, that must be bottom. I came out of the shaft, into the light and landed on my butt on the floor.

On the floor of the hallway, with Dad behind me whooping loudly. I had completed the twelfth and final test. I passed the Trials.

Dad grabbed me in a big hug. He picked me up, swung me around, and then set me down. "You did it, Bella! You did it!"

Dad walked over to the wall where the slits were. There was a stream of paper coming out of the larger one and Dad pulled the paper up and was reading it. I looked around the hallway in awe. I was finished.

The timer in the middle of the room had disappeared. All the doors were closed and plain wood again. "You have a remaining time of three weeks, four days, eighteen hours, thirty-four minutes and fifty-two point nine seconds. Third best time in the history of the Trials. Third!" Dad looked at me. "Wow, Bella!"

I couldn't stop smiling. I was exhausted, dirty, smelly, but so happy. Behind us, I could hear the large metal slabs surrounding the barn banging open. We could leave. We could go home. I could shower. Oh, a shower... I would stand under the hot water for hours.

Part Three: The Trials of the Gods

The barn door slammed open. Two large women walked in and yelled, "Stop!" I suddenly could not move. At all. I couldn't blink. I tried to move my eyes to look at Dad but they wouldn't cooperate. The women were right in front of me so I got a good look at them. Tall, maybe seven feet each. White. Not Caucasian white but their skin was a watered-down milk color. They were wearing armor from their shoulders to their feet. White hair flowed out of their heads down to their knees and seemed to move with its own gentle breeze. They had wings, six of them, also pure white. They hurt to look at, but I couldn't look away or close my eyes.

One of the women moved out of my field of view towards where Dad was. She came back carrying the paper with my results and Dad's bio-card. The two leaned close to each other, and talked for a moment. They finished and the one with the paper walked back over towards Dad. The other one walked towards me.

"You are to be placed under confinement pending a trial for the violation of multiple Joint Commission Statutes. Any attempt to flee will be met with immortality ending force. Any utterances or thoughts can be held against you. As a partial or full human, you have the right to declare a faith belief and request examination for that faith. If found to be valid, and that faith has a defender, you have the right to ask for that defender to support you. As a partial or full human, you also are entitled to a guide of your choosing to explain your charges and the process of the trial. The guide may not be your co-conspirator, and must be your defender, if applicable. Do you understand these rights and responsibilities as presented to you?"

No, I didn't understand. What was happening? Were we being arrested?

The white angel-looking woman spoke again, standing very close to me, looking into my face. "What part of the statutes of pre-trial confinement do you not understand?" Could she hear me thinking? "Yes," she replied. "I can hear your acknowledgements of me."

OK, I understand those rights you gave me, but I don't understand why you are here and what is happening.

"Are you electing to have a guide?" she asked.

Yes. Yes, a guide please.

"Do you profess a faith?" she asked.

No, no faith. Who could be a guide for me? Who did I know here? There was the flaming guy, Bob from Accounting, but I never actually talked to him. For all I knew he was a boob. Jim! Dad's secretary Jim. I choose Jim.

"James Monroe from Human Resources will be contacted for you and will meet you at the confinement facility," she stated blandly.

Human Resources? No, the Jim from Dad's office, who offered me brunch on that Thursday I went to Dad's work with him.

"Your father's office is called Human Resources. That Jim is James Monroe." Her bland voice had a tinge of annoyance. "You will now be released from the bonds enough to transport. Do not struggle or attempt to flee."

Dad! Dad! Where is my father? I felt the bonds loosen and blinked hard, my eyes watering a little. I tried to look around for him, but he was nowhere. He and the other white woman were gone.

"Your father has already been transported to the containment facility. You will not be allowed to converse with him until after testimony has been taken and then only if the commission allows." The angel woman walked behind me and pushed on my back. "Walk."

I stiffly walked forward, out the door of the barn and into the idyllic field.

"Stop." The bland voice of the angel woman came from behind me.

I stopped and nothing happened for about thirty seconds. Then the world twisted weirdly. When everything snapped back into place, I was standing on concrete in front of a white metal door. The door had a small window near the top, well above my head, covered with white, powder-coated mesh. At the bottom of the door was a small flap. On the center of the door were words and numbers painted in black.

Human Confinement
1108–367

The angel woman was still behind me. She reached around me and pushed the door open. "Walk," she intoned.

I walked into the room. The woman pulled the door shut and I head it click. I didn't even have to try it to know it was locked solid. I looked around the room I was in. The walls were concrete blocks painted white. The floor was unpainted concrete. The ceiling was one of those cheap white drop ceilings with one lone fluorescent light. The ceiling was at least ten feet up, even standing on furniture, I wouldn't have been able to touch it. At least the fluorescent light wasn't blinking.

There was a bed in the far-left corner of the room that looked as if it was screwed into the floor. Single bed, metal frame with wires wrapping back and forth to make a box spring. At the foot of the bed was a blue-ticked mattress folded into thirds. There was a pillow next to it and a sheet and blanket folded on top of the pillow.

In the far-right corner, there was a toilet attached to the wall. The top of the toilet, instead of being the tank, was a sink basin with a spicket and one twisty handle to turn on and off the water. Next to the toilet, there was a drain in the floor about the size of my fist. Attached to the wall, just above head height, was a shower head. the shower head would have been too low for someone like Dad, but was probably an OK height for me. Halfway between the shower head and the floor was a twisty handle just like on the sink.

I turned around to look at the wall with the door in it. The door was facing opposite the toilet and shower. In the other corner, opposite the bed, was a desk and chair. The desk was an old-fashioned metal desk with two drawers down the right side, screwed into the floor the same height the bed was. The chair matched the desk, metal with no padding on the seat. On the desk were several items. There was a toothbrush and hairbrush, both new in wrapper. There was a travel-sized toothpaste, bar soap, and two small bottles that I assumed were shampoo and conditioner. Next to them was a full roll of toilet paper. Next to that was a stack of fabric.

I walked over to see what was in the stack. Bra, panties, socks, shirt and pants, all in a dark blue. There was also a towel and wash cloth, both blue. Under all that was a cream canvas bag with the words *Laundry 1108-367* stamped on it.

I opened the drawers on the desk. The top one had a yellow legal pad and one pen. The bottom was empty.

Next to the desk was a metal trash can. Beneath the desk was a pair of dark blue slip-on canvas shoes.

Someone banged on the door. "Remove all personal items, including clothing, and place them in the laundry bag," a rough, disembodied voice said. "Then slide the bag through the slot in the door."

Prison. This was prison. Just like every movie on TV. My mind couldn't focus. I was in prison.

Maybe I was still in the Trials. The last test had said to go to Hell. Well, if prison wasn't Hell, what was? Maybe I really did fall through the trapdoor to Hell and this is just what it looked like to me. My mind didn't really believe me, but trying to find a reasonable answer to how I ended up in a place like this helped clear my mind enough to get me moving. Not sure I wanted that disembodied voice coming in here. It sounded scary.

I tried to get myself motivated by pulling up my Heka. I felt for it. Nothing. There was no ice and warm in my belly. All that was there was emptiness. How did they do that? If Heka was everywhere, and everything, how was It not here?

Maybe I was just tired. I slipped off my tattered and dirty clothes, threw them in the laundry bag. Goodbye Converse shoes. They were ragged and filthy, but they had done the job and I was sad to see them go. I grabbed the toiletries and walked over to the shower, turning the handle all the way on. A slow, weak stream of water came out of the shower head. Lukewarm at best and with low water pressure. Better than a poke in the eye. I had hoped for a steamy hot shower for hours. Instead, I got tepid water and a thirty-minute limit before it just cut off. But I was clean and that felt infinitely better. I peed then. I did not realize I had to pee so bad, holy crap. Oh yeah, I hadn't peed in almost nine weeks. Then I brushed my teeth and hair. I kept my ponytail band. Screw 'em.

I dressed in the clothes left for me, wiped up the wet room with the towel and shoved the laundry bag, the wet towel and wash cloth through the flap in the door. Then I put the other toiletries away in the bottom drawer of the desk. I kept the toilet paper in the sink. I made the bed up and laid down. Not a bad bed for what it was. Not great, but not bad.

I never meant to fall asleep. I guess my body just needed it after everything. But I woke up to the flap in the door opening and a food tray being slid through it. Meatloaf, green beans, mashed potatoes, butter, orange juice, and a small bit of chocolate pudding. The food didn't taste too awful, so I scarfed it down and pushed the empty tray back through the flap.

I don't know how long I was in that cell alone. I know I was brought food six times and fresh clothes and towels twice. But there were never any changes, like the lights going on or off, and there were no windows to the outside, so it could have been one day or twenty years. I spent most of the time sleeping. When I couldn't sleep any more, I would count the number of blocks on each wall. The two short walls had seventy-two bricks each and the two long ones had ninety bricks each. Sometimes I would draw on the legal pad, but that got boring quickly. I did anything I could to try not to think about Dad and where he was. And I most definitely did not think about Mom. What did she know? Nope, I was not thinking about her.

At some point after I had finished my sixth meal, the door unlocked and a man walked inside looking through some papers. It was Jim. I had forgotten all about him.

"Good morning," Jim said. "I am James Monroe. Apparently, you requested me as your guide through the trial."

"Yeah," I replied. "Hey, Jim."

"Do I know you?" he asked.

"Um, kind of." Maybe he didn't remember me. Why would he? "I came with Dad to his work for two days."

He looked up from his paper. "AnnaBella Cain. Oh, yeah. Nick did have that groupie for two days a while ago. That was you?" He looked around and whistled. "Wow, gotta say. Never thought Ol' Nick was messing around like that. But to have brought you right into work? Ballsy."

I had so many questions. "Jim," I started. "Where is my dad?"

Jim turned formal again. He sat down in the metal chair. I sat up on the bed and turned to him. "Nick Cain was charged with one count unauthorized procreation, one count deceptive practices, one count human testing, and one count failure to report Heka misuse. He had his trial and has been sentenced to..." Jim flipped though his papers. "One-thousand-year ban from corporeal form, one-thousand-year ban from earth, infinite ban from areas unrelated to his living and working environments. Wow, he got off easy."

Dad was banned from going to earth for a thousand years? How could he see me then? If I got out of here, that is.

"Mom," I said. "What about my mom?"

Jim reviewed the paperwork again, responding, "The human, Julia McIntosh, was not charged with any crimes. I believe a review of the circumstances showed she did not know the mating was forbidden." Jim looked up and realized that had not been what I was asking. He spoke nicer this time, more friendly. "As far as I know, your mom still thinks you are on summer break with your dad. You are not slotted to start school for another week."

Jim gave me a moment to feel the relief that at least, with everything else being crazy, Mom was not worried about me. Then he continued, "Now, we need to talk about your trial. You have been charged with one count of deceptive practices, one count unauthorized human testing, Heka misuse, one count Trial Arena misuse, and a bunch of other tiny charges that basically sum up to you were a child of a coordinator and a human and no one said you could be born much less know about all this stuff. Most of this stuff is frivolous and should only be a slap on the wrist, but the Heka misuse and deception, they carry some pretty hefty penalties. You could be sentenced to human death and judgement by your faith."

Jim looked up at me again. He saw that he was going way over my head. He sighed. "OK, let's start over. How much do you understand about where you are and what you did? You visited your dad's courtroom so I assume you get the basic way it all works. Do you understand what the purpose of the Trials in Area One are for?"

"To see how much Heka I have and if I can use It well enough to work with Dad," I replied.

"Pretty much," Jim agreed. "There is a little bit more to it, though. Your score on the Trials places you in the Commission. Low scores or failure become completely human, whether Heka made or human born. Mid-range scores become coordinators, like me and your dad. There is a whole hierarchy to that system, but it doesn't matter right now. The usual people to score in that range are those Heka made to be coordinators, their human born children, and a couple of prophets or oracles that formed when Heka decided to give regular humans a super dose. Most people who pass the Trials end up in this category. High enough score, you become a demi-god. Get an even higher score, you become a god. Only people who have ever scored that high were either made by the Heka as a god or were the child of a god with a coordinator or human. Making children with humans has been outlawed for thousands of years, except by special dispensation. Even then, those children have not been allowed to do the Trials but only allowed to become defense workers for the humans at their death. Heka seemed to be following our rules and hasn't made a prophet or oracle of the testable level since we outlawed human testing. Following along so far?"

I nodded that I was. Jim continued. "Now there is you. You dad broke the rules and made a kid, aka you. Your mom has been cleared of any wrongdoing, so pretty much any of the charges against you for being created can be waived since you couldn't control being born."

Made sense. Jim was still talking. "Then your dad brought you up here and told you about everything. Not strictly illegal, but probably not cool since you were an unauthorized child. The charges for that stuff will most likely be waived too."

Jim took a breath, and continued. "Now we get to the Trials. Your dad used his bio-card to start the Trials for you. Did you know he wasn't supposed to?"

"No," I answered. "Dad just did stuff. And told me go. So, I went."

"OK, there may be some room there," Jim told me. "You are charged with deceptive practices for using your dad's bio-card to start the Trials. If he never told you that wasn't how it worked, and you had no other way of knowing, never witnessed a Trials run before, you could get found innocent of that. Next, you are charged with unauthorized human testing. Did you know that humans were not supposed to go through the Trials?"

I thought about that little extra plate of writing on the plaque in the hallway of the Trials Arena. I told Jim the truth. "There was something written on the plaque in the Trials Arena, but Dad had told me that coordinators and humans could make kids with special permission. I thought that he had that for me, and that the special permission meant he could take me through the Trials. He made it sound like all human-coordinator kids had to go through the Trials."

Jim rubbed his hand over his face. "They might accept that answer, they might not. You saw the warning and ignored it in favor of your father's instructions. Try it as a defense." He sighed and shook his head. "Now, Trials Arena misuse. That charge shouldn't be there along with the human testing. They should have done one or the other. I really think they only threw that in there because they are mad at you."

"Mad at me?" I questioned Jim. "Why?"

"Remember how I explained the scoring? That children of coordinators and humans would be placed into their position in the Commission as a coordinator or made just a human by their Trials results? And that the only people who scored high enough to be a god or demi-god were either Heka-made for that position or their children?" I nodded. Jim took a breath, then said the rest in a rush. "That was true. Was. Now there is you. You scored insanely high. Like higher than all but five people ever. Ever. Every god, demi-god, coordinator, everyone but the five original gods from the paleolithic period who were the gods who made the Trials Arena. They made the arena, so of course they did really well. You did almost as well as they did and better than literally everyone else. And you did it faster than three of those paleolithic gods. By right, your score makes you capable of being a top-tier god with a worldwide religion."

Jim gave me a moment to let that sink in. Woah. "How did Dad score?" I asked.

Jim looked at me. "I don't know exactly, but based on his position, and the fact that he was made not born, I would guess in the mid-tier coordinator range. Basically, if we say your dad scored at the bottom fifty per cent, you score by comparison would be the top one per cent. Your dad, me, hell most everyone you have seen so far up here, are burger flippers while you are Stephen Hawking. At best, Hercules who made the Trials famous, would just barely be in the top seventy-five per cent compared to your score."

OK, that was a pretty good analogy. It didn't make me any less overwhelmed by my results.

"And that is where the last issue comes in," Jim said. "The Heka misuse. I am sure you know where that charge came from."

Test five. The timer. Yeah, I knew. And I was guilty.

Jim saw my face drop. "You have to understand," he said this very tenderly. "Thirty-seven humans died when you did that, over two hundred were hospitalized."

I stammered at Jim, "But the Heka said…"

He had been looking away from me, as if to hide from my shame, but when I used the word *said* with the word *Heka*, his head snapped towards me and he jumped from his chair, making it fall over. "Stop talking. Right now. If the Heka spoke to you, and that is such a major if, I do not want to know. I want nothing to do with that. That would be so far above my pay grade. And guide rules or no guide rules, I am not touching that. Tell it to the courts if you want but not me."

Well, that wasn't an intense reaction or anything. The Heka spoke to me and told me I did not supersede Its power. Blaming me for those deaths was wrong. I mean, if they really were my fault, OK. I accept what I did was so wrong. So, so very wrong. But the Heka said It was going to right everything. I looked at Jim and shook my head. That was something between me and the court, I guess.

Jim shook off the deep apprehension at the mention of the Heka talking with someone. He righted the chair, sat down again and continued explaining my charges. "Now, since you had a misuse of Heka there, the courts believe you may have abused the Heka throughout the entire Trials and have moved to have your results nullified." I started to protest and Jim stopped me. "If you didn't, the review will show that, but they could possibly invalidate your results on that one instance alone. But misuse of Heka does not just invalidate your results. It carries the weight of a punishment up to and including death. This will be the crux of your trial."

Jim and I sat in silence for a while so I could absorb all this new information. After a time, he slapped his knees and said, "Whelp," as if we hadn't just been talking about me receiving the death penalty. "The Commission has convened to begin the trial. Since you are part coordinator, the trial will consist of the Full Commission. Ready?"

"Wait," I exclaimed. "My trial is now? Right now?"

"Yes," Jim told me. "They are waiting."

Jim stood, and in shock, I stood too. I followed Jim out of my cell door and the world twisted. When it settled, we were at Dad's office, in the hallway by his courtroom. We walked past his courtroom door to the silver door at the end. Jim pushed the door open and we walked in.

Ever watched a State of the Union address on C-SPAN or had a tour of the DC government buildings? Remember how the Senate chamber looks? This room looked like that only a lot, lot bigger. Instead of holding a few hundred people, it held thousands. Every god and demi-god that ever had or ever would exist had a seat in there. As I walked past, most were milling around, chatting with each other. In the second story, there were all the coordinators, prophets and oracles.

As I made my way to the floor, Jim explained, "You sit there at the table on the right. There is no prosecutor for a trial like this. The whole Commission acts as both the prosecutor and the judges in a way, so the table on the left will be empty. At the judge's table is the speaker. They run the show, translating the votes of the Commission into verdicts and then decide the punishments or rewards. We vote on a new speaker every hundred years. A god can only hold the position once every ten thousand years, and demi-gods cannot hold it."

I looked at the judge's table. There was a slender woman with a shaved head, wearing a handmade leather bra and loincloth and lots of necklaces, arm and wrist bracelets. Her ears were pierced in every conceivable spot and each hole had an earring. Her nose was also pierced and there was a small nose ring in it that had a tiny chain running from the nose ring to one of her earrings in her left ear. She was very black. So black she almost seemed to have streaks of purple. As I looked at her, a necklace of blue beads appeared around her neck. She fingered the necklace for a moment, smiling and looking off into nowhere, then went back to a very serious expression as she looked back at the papers on her desk. I realized as I watched that she must have been a goddess for some tribe somewhere and one of her followers had just given her the necklace as an offering. She must have accepted the offering and was now wearing the necklace with pride. I wondered if that was where all the rest of her jewelry came from, because so much of it was really pretty.

Jim had still been talking as I watched the speaker. "You can ask for video or document reviews anytime. The court can refuse, and you can challenge. You might lose the challenge though so don't do it just to buy time. It looks bad and doesn't do you any favors. But if you really feel a review of something might make things clearer, ask for it."

We arrived at my table. "This is where I leave you," Jim told me. "I will be sitting up there." He pointed to the second-tier seating. I followed where he was pointing. Looking through the crowd, I happened to see Bob from Accounting. He wasn't screaming and he only glowed a little with fire. He must have had his coffee already. I kept scanning the crowd.

"Your father is not allowed in the courtroom," Jim told me. "Sorry. Just remember to be respectful and ask questions if you don't understand something. You may be on trial for committing some crimes, but you have the right to defend yourself and how can you do that if you don't understand what is happening? You won't get any leniency for your actions, but the speaker is a fair one, she will not punish you only because you don't understand the way the court works. Good luck." Then, he walked away and I was on my own.

The speaker banged her gavel, and everyone started shuffling around towards their designated seats. By the time she finished banging her gavel, everyone including me, had sat down. "AnnaBella Cain versus the Commission," she began. "Trial one-one-zero-eight-three-six-seven. Ms Cain, would you like to claim a faith and a defense actor?"

Timidly, I spoke. "No, ma'am."

"Ms Cain," she replied. "Please speak up and into the microphone."

I pulled the microphone on the table closer to me, and repeated myself. "No, ma'am."

The speaker set aside some papers. "Then we shall convene. For your information, Ms Cain, you are to address me as Ms Speaker."

I cleared my throat. "I apologize, Ms Speaker."

She ignored my apology. "The court accepts that the charges have been read. Does Ms Cain wish a full reading?"

I cleared my throat again. Nerves had made it go dry. "No, Ms Speaker."

A glass of water appeared on the table next to me. I'm not saying it appeared by magic or something, someone could have slipped it there without me seeing. I was that distracted. I took a sip and felt better.

The speaker continued while I drank. "In the interest of justice, the court submits that all charges against Ms Cain pertaining to actions by or for her that happened prior to June tenth of her seventeenth year be dismissed. Does any on the Commission disagree?"

The speaker waited. Some people were talking or shuffling papers but no one responded in a vocal way. "So decided." The speaker banged her gavel. "Charges one to fourteen dismissed. Now to the charge of deceptive practices, Ms Cain, how do you plead?"

"Not guilty, Ms Speaker," I said, my voice working a lot better.

The speaker waited. She seemed like I should be saying something else, so I said what Jim said, "I had never witnessed the Trials being run before, and I was never shown or explained any rules concerning the use of a bio-card in the Trials." I didn't know what else to say, except, "I didn't even know what that badge thing was until I read the plaque in the arena. I thought it was just a fancy work badge like lots of humans use to get into their work. Like a hotel key or something."

The speaker stared at me. "Does anyone have knowledge of hotel keys or work badges like Ms Cain talks of?"

Someone way in the back spoke up. "Ms Speaker, I have used such hotel keys. I could very much see a human mistaking a bio-card for one. For the humans, they are just a touchless key, transferrable from one to another at will."

"Thank you, Cronus," the speaker said. "In light of this human misconception, I would move for a preemptory finding. All those who find Ms Cain guilty of deceptive practices say aye."

The speaker and I waited. No one said anything. "In that case, on the count of deceptive practices, this court finds the defendant, Ms Cain, not guilty."

One down. I felt hot and sticky. I took another sip of water, but it didn't help.

"On the count of unauthorized human testing." The speaker moved on. "How do you plead?"

"Not guilty, Ms Speaker," I said. "Dad never told me I wasn't authorized. He said having babies with humans required authorization, so I assumed my dad got that to have me. And the way he spoke about the Trials, I thought everyone who was anything other than full human had to do them."

"Ms Cain," the speaker asked. "Did you not just admit to having read the plaque in the Trials Arena?"

"Yes, Ms Speaker." I faltered a little here. Nerves. "I read it."

"And did you also read the addendum on the bottom of that plaque?" she questioned.

"Yes, Ms Speaker." Uh oh.

"And do you now," the speaker was speaking very slowly and carefully, "or did you then consider yourself to be human, Ms Cain?"

Really, uh oh. I spoke softly, "Yes."

The speaker got a little more forceful. "Speak up, Ms Cain."

I cleared my throat again, kind of freaking out. "Yes, Ms Speaker. I considered myself human at that time."

"Then you should have been aware you were not allowed in the Trials while they were operational. Do you have anything more to say in your defense, Ms Cain?" The speaker was not being nice at all with this.

I could have placed the blame on Dad then. I could have, but I didn't. The words wouldn't come out. This was the lie, the secret. It all hit me then. The lie I almost pulled out of him. I was unauthorized, made in secret and he was breaking twenty million rules by having me do all this. I was not supposed to be, I shouldn't exist. And I should never have been within spitting distance of the Trials Arena, much less in them, doing them. A tear rolled down my cheek and I wiped it away.

The speaker did not care about my existential crisis. "Ms Cain, your failure to respond is taken as a negative response. With no other defense offered, I move to vote. All those who find Ms Cain guilty of unauthorized human testing, say aye."

The courtroom resounded with 'ayes' from every direction. "All those who find Ms Cain innocent of the charge, say nay," the speaker directed.

A scattered few 'nays' came from here or there. It was a handful at most, out of thousands.

The speaker banged her gavel. "The ayes have it. Next charge, Trial Arena misuse. Per Section forty-seven, subsection eight of the Trial Arena bylaws, misuse of the Trial Arena occurs when the tested individual purposely deceives the arena by flagrant misuse of Heka, purposeful dodging of test requirements, or any destructive actions meant to invalidate or falsify a test result. These actions must happen in at least six out of the twelve tests. Have the records of the Trials been reviewed?"

A god near me stood up. "Yes, Ms Speaker," they said. "The records indicate deception only happened in one of the twelves tests. The other tests, the defendant used... erm, creative solutions, but none were outside the bounds of the test or meant to deceive or manipulate them. In fact, the arena scored the creative solutions higher, and gave extra points for..." The god flipped through a few pages. "Thinking outside the box and using surroundings in unconventional ways."

"Thank you, Pan," the speaker said. "In light of this, the court has not proved a sufficient burden to charge Ms Cain with Trial Arena misuse. The charge will be struck from the records as invalid."

The whole place erupted. Gods were yelling at the speaker and each other. People were flipping through papers and some gods were looking at the balcony, pointing at coordinators, saying things. The coordinator would then run from the room to get whatever the god had directed them to.

The speaker stood and banged her gavel over and over, yelling, "Quiet! Quiet! Members of the Commission, show some decorum!" The speaker banged the gavel again. The Commission settled down slowly and the speaker waited for them all to be reseated. "Listen, I understand your frustration," she said, being a whole lot kinder to them than she ever had been to me. "But we created the Trials Arena to work a very specific way. We created the laws about the arena the way we did after careful thought and consideration. It is exactly cases like this that prove why we need these rules. So, now we either abide by the rules we made, or throw the whole thing away into Chaos. Do you want to go back to Chaos running things?" The speaker waited. Other than a few murmurings here and there, no one said anything. "I didn't think so. The ruling stands, unchallengeable in perpetuity. If any of you believe AnnaBella Cain's actions have presented unforeseen consequences that mean the rules of the arena need to be altered, you can write up a proposition stating so and read it out at the next Commission meeting. But even if that proposition ends in a rule change, it will not be retroactively applied to Ms Cain. She can only be charged with crimes based on the rules as they stood at the time of her actions, not what we change them to later."

The speaker banged her gavel one more time then sat back. Even she needed to take a moment before moving on. The next charge, I knew, was the big one. Heka misuse. This one was the real reason we were here. Well, that and the fact that I made everyone in this room except five look stupid.

The speaker took a deep breath and leaned back towards the microphone. "For the charge of misuse of Heka, Ms Cain, how do you plead?"

"Um," I started. "Ms Speaker, I am not sure how to answer this."

The speaker looked confused. "Ms Cain," she replied, "you either think you are guilty of this crime or that you are innocent. What do you not understand?"

"Ms Speaker," I countered. "I believe there were… what's the word? Extenuating. Yeah, extenuating circumstances."

The speaker tapped her pen for a moment, considering this. "Continue," she said.

I sat up a little straighter in my chair. It was important that I got this right the first time. I had to think about what to say very carefully. "I was told that time worked differently in the tests." Dad. Dad told me that. "But I was never fully explained how time worked to know what different meant. I know what I did in the fifth test was wrong, but I only know that *now*. At the time, when I started the test, you have to consider all I had experienced with time. I had been in the regular world, seeing time as a clock. Sometimes that clock seemed to go slowly, sometimes fast, but always forward. In Dad's courtroom, I saw time seem to stop. We went into his work in the morning, like eight a.m. There was a trial for hundreds of people. That should have taken days or weeks. But when we left Dad's work, it was only five p.m., dinner time."

I stopped and took a breath. Take your time to explain, Bella. "In the first four tests, time seemed to jump forward, with things that should have taken a few hours taking days. I only asked time to do something I had seen it do before. No one told me that the way time worked in one spot was connected to the way time worked in another and that time, the way it worked in each of those places, had to stay the same in relation to each other.

"I am incredibly sorry for what I did, and had I known then what I do now, I never would have done that. I am incredibly sorry that my actions caused the gods, coordinators, and humans pain and suffering and that some people died. But I cannot be held responsible for what no one told me."

The speaker listened to my speech. Then she smiled, almost sadly. "Ms Cain, while I appreciate what you have said, and your remorse has been noted, you are not being charged with misuse of time. You are charged with the misuse of Heka. You took your Heka outside of yourself, twisted it inside out, and changed its form. Do you understand the charge?"

Now I got it. They weren't upset about what I did to time. Well, maybe they were a little, but that is not what I was in trouble for. They were mad I could bend Heka, maybe in a way they couldn't. "Yes, Ms Speaker," I said into the microphone.

"Then how do you plead?" she asked again.

I sat up straight. If they were just mad that I did something they couldn't, that was no reason to sentence me to death. If what I did was wrong, if I mishandled the Heka, wasn't it the Heka who should deal with that? And hadn't the Heka already dealt with it right there in the Trials Area after test five? This court didn't have the right to say whether what I did was against the rules for a thing, being, power they could not even define much less explain, especially when that thing had already made Its own decisions about what I did. Talk to me about the lives lost, OK. But not what I did with something bigger than all of them, that created all of them.

I spoke firmly now, "Not guilty, Ms Speaker."

She wasn't expecting that. Neither was anyone else. The room broke out in whispers. The speaker sputtered into the microphone, "Defense?"

I turned it around. "I need no defense. You have no charge. I used the Heka as I could. To claim I misused the Heka, to have that as a crime, you must first define exactly what the Heka is, how It works and how It does not. You must show that you have a set of rules from the Heka Itself telling you what is and is not allowed. Can you do that, Ms Speaker?"

The speaker turned pale. She knew they couldn't. It was like humans defining what the gods were, Dad had said, only way bigger. The whole Commission was in an uproar. People were yelling that I was Chaos itself. Others were saying that I was being impertinent. One person actually said they thought an actual demon had been discovered, humans had been right all along, they do exist.

But others were sitting in awe. Some of them had seen what I was saying and they were supporting me, saying to others, "Prove that her Heka doesn't work like that, both inside and outside". Some were wondering if all the gods everywhere had missed how the Heka actually worked this whole time. Even if Heka Itself maybe wouldn't want It used that way, it was up to the Heka, not them, to decide how to deal with Its misuse. Others were just astounded by the vile things others were saying about me and were telling others to try the case not the person, she still is a living being, deserving of respect.

The speaker was weakly banging her gavel, trying to bring back some sense of order, but her heart really wasn't in it. I tried to speak again, but it took a few times for people to settle down enough to hear me.

Finally, the room quietened enough for me to speak. There were still loud murmurs but mostly everyone was listening. "Ms Speaker," I began. "Really, the whole Commission, I have a question. Even if, let's say, I did use the Heka wrong, can you convict me of the crime if the Heka Itself told me that It forgave me for my mistake with the timer? Wouldn't the Heka have the final say on that, the same way each individual god has the final say over the rules their worshippers must follow and other gods or humans are not allowed to intervene?"

The entire room went silent. Not the silent it had been before with rustling papers and whispers, but so silent it might have been empty. The speaker tried to talk.

"Are you attempting to assert you spoke with..." the speaker's voice cracked and she tried again. "You spoke with the Heka? Do you... have proof?"

"Ask my father, he was there," I said. Then, as an afterthought, I added, "Oh, and if you don't believe him right now, check the records. The Heka reset the clock some after I had a whole nervous breakdown about possibly having killed people with the timer issue. It forgave me, told me everyone was fine, and let me collect myself before turning the timer back to when I exited test five."

The god Pan found himself in the eyes of the speaker and literally everyone else in the room. He shuffled through papers. "Ms Cain, um, her explanation would account for a few inconsistencies we saw in the records. After test five, Ms Cain is recorded to have had a conversation with... the report left this field blank. It had noted her conversing with her father under many instances, and the exact words said were recorded as normal, but at this moment the record just says, 'Conversation, indistinguishable, with', and then moves to the next line where it records Ms Cain causing self-mutilations on the door of the arena. The records indicate that the injuries were removed, not healed by the arena but removed by a yet-again unnamed source. Finally, the times recorded for each line were consistent, but after her injuries were, um, removed, the timer moves back in time with no explanation given except, 'Timer correction authorized'. No other irregularities were found in the records, and since they were during the same period as the test five, they were counted as part of that arena misuse charge and ignored in further charges."

The speaker preemptively banged her gavel. The gods had started to rumble like they were going to go nuts again. But the speaker banged her gavel. "Stop!" she yelled. "Let me think." The room went quiet, the normal quiet with rustling papers and whispers. The speaker sat with her head in her hands for a long time.

Finally, the speaker addressed the Commission again. "I want to preface this with a mandate," she began slowly. "Anyone, god, coordinator, or human who yells out from this point forward during the trial of AnnaBella Cain will be immediately removed by the Avenging Women." At this she waved at the door, and the very white angel looking women who had escorted me to prison came into the room. "They will be charged will disruption of the Commission and jailed for one hundred years."

The speaker stopped and took a deep breath. "AnnaBella Cain, on the charge of unauthorized human testing, you have been found guilty. On the charge of

Heka misuse, the court finds the proceedings to be a mistrial." There were gasps all around the room that quickly silenced themselves. "So you understand, Ms Cain," she continued. "There has never been a mistrial in the history of the Commission. We did not have such a thing until I just did it now. But here we are. You are right that we, the Commission, cannot charge you with misuse of something we cannot explain how we use. Especially since it seems like there was some sort of intervention in the Trials Arena that was... well, beyond the power of the gods and there is no way for us to confirm if that in fact was the Heka." The speaker seemed as if she wanted to say something else, weighed her words, and decided against saying it.

She shook her head, took a deep breath, and started to speak. Again, she stopped herself and shook her head, deciding not to say what she was going to say. While the speaker debated with herself on how to continue, I felt the tension in the room climbing. Small glances around showed me several gods who were squirming and whispering, fighting the urge to blurt out however they felt.

Finally, the speaker started talking again. "Ms Cain, with the power given to me by the position of the speaker of the Commission, I authorize punishment for your crime, potentially crimes, by the gods of your express faith, in respect for your partial humanness. Their punishments are limited to one of the following choices.

"Choice One: you are to be stripped of your Heka. All but a normal human amount will be blocked to your access. You will be sent back to your mother as a full human. Your memory of these events will be wiped by use of coma. Your mother will believe you and your father were in a car accident where he perished and you were left gravely injured. Upon your healing, neither she nor you will remember knowing of his position as a coordinator. You will live out your days as a human, with a human mother and a deceased human father.

"Choice Two: you are stripped of your humanness. You will become a full coordinator. You will be denied the god status achieved by your Trials results and will be placed in the position of prosecuting coordinator, to work with your father. Your mother will be allowed to believe both you and your father perished in the car accident. She will be allowed all comforts the gods of her faith allow for the mourning as normal. You will not, under any circumstances be allowed on earth or to interact with humans except as required by your duties as prosecutor for eternity."

The speaker took a breath. No one in the Commission room spoke. Most people didn't move, for fear of the speaker. Her Heka was exuding from her as she spoke down the sentencing. She tried to reign in back in, but it was taking a strong act of will. She was glowing and several of her necklaces seemed to actually be hovering just above her skin rather than lying on it. I focused on those necklaces because nothing in my mind was working. Not the death penalty for me, but basically for one of my parents? I either lose my mom forever and she thinks I am dead, or lose my dad forever and I think he is dead. That's the choice? I cannot tell you what I was thinking at this point because, even now, I have no idea what to think. No matter which way it went, someone was going to end up hurt and mourning a loss.

While I tried to become un-numb, the speaker had called out, "Malachi."

The very, very old man who was the examiner in Dad's courtroom shuffled out. "Ms Speaker?"

The speaker pointed at me. "Please determine the defendant's faith."

Malachi looked at me for a long time, then said, "AnnaBella Cain. Humanity."

The speaker questioned Malachi. "What do you mean humanity?"

Malachi turned to her and explained, "Ms Cain is not an atheist. She has always accepted the idea of a god or gods existing, so does not qualify under the atheist ruling. She is not agnostic as she was not confused by a choice or questioning which god or gods may be right. She understands completely that they all are right and wrong equally for all. She understands this at a level transcending human comprehension, so does not qualify under the agnostic ruling.

"Ms Cain, though, has complete faith in basic human decency. Her faith, truly and deeply, lies with humans and their ability to do what is right, be what is kind, and decide her own future and theirs without god interference. She has faith that, given the opportunity, humans could potentially rely on the Heka in Its infiniteness to make proper decisions and even believes that the gods make humans worse at points, not better. Therefore, her faith is humanity. Her judges should be humans."

The speaker looked up and sighed. "So be it," she said and banged her gavel.

And this is that. They determined that I should write my story and give it to you. Here it is, in a way humans could handle it. As a novel you picked up in a bookstore or library or garage sale. Now, you have to decide. I have been found guilty of unauthorized human testing. Am I guilty of Heka misuse? Or am I just Heka-gifted with a deeper understanding than even a god or coordinator? You have to make that choice. Which punishment do I deserve? Should I be stripped of my humanness and made a coordinator? Or stripped of my Heka and made a human? Malachi said my faith is humanity, and I think he is right. I trust you to make the right call. As a coordinator, I could help humans to bear the weight of what their lives were and get the right justice from their gods. I would be fair and kind. As a human, who knows what I could do? Human lives are so changeable. I could be anything. So, you must decide. But dear reader, you and many others like you need to choose quickly. I beg you, please. As I wait, I am held in cell one-one-zero-eight-three-six-seven. You don't need to do anything to make your choice known. Just decide and believe it totally. The Heka will give the gods your answer. And the Heka will enforce the gods following your choice. When enough humans have voiced their choice, I will be let go to serve my penance as the majority decided. So, make your choice and then give this book to a friend, your family, a neighbor, and let them choose too, so I may be freed that much sooner. Human or coordinator? Earth or the heavens? Mom or Dad? Make your choice.

Thank you.